Secret Dreams

by

JoMarie DeGioia

PUBLISHED BY:

Bailey Park Publishing

ISBN: 978-1-944181-34-5

Secret Dreams

Book Two of the
Cloud Canyon Series

by

JoMarie DeGioia

Chapter 1

Cloud Canyon, California

Chloe Butler heard a masculine murmur, followed by a throaty laugh, and caught her breath.

Jeez, has it been that long?

She wiped her damp palms on the front of her apron. The Cloud Café, hers and hers alone for the past four years, was as well known for its charm as it was for Tom the cook's mouthwatering food. The place was filled with an eclectic mix of mismatched chairs and tables with folk art and antique signs on the walls which she had hand-picked herself. The utensils on the tables were as mismatched as the furniture, but heavy and well-made. Everything here was serviceable and pleasing to the eye, and it was little wonder that the Cloud Café was so popular with the locals.

She'd built this business way, way up from the greasy-spoon diner that had previously occupied the space, and she had good reason to be proud of it even if some days she felt a little bit overworked. Sure, the café did brisk business for breakfast and lunch today as usual, but that didn't explain the flush she felt on her cheeks and across her chest. Heck, she wasn't a silly teenager. But today the sight of the blond guy nuzzling his female companion at the table in the corner caused an odd fluttering in her belly.

Why should she have such a reaction? He was just a stranger, as was the girl he was nuzzling. Sure, he looked a little like someone. Someone she hadn't thought about in years. Well, in months anyway. Her reaction must just be hormones. It couldn't have anything to do with her own dismal love life. And no, her flush had nothing to do with a certain blond jerk from her past.

"Abstinence makes the heart grow fonder," she muttered as she refilled coffee cups on the nearest table.

"What's that, dear?"

Chloe started, then smiled at the three elderly Bennet sisters seated at their usual table. "Nothing."

"You could always feel the heat between those two," one of the sisters, Charlotte, said.

"Hmm?" She glanced at the stranger as he left his money on the table and walked out with his girlfriend. The bell on the door signaled their exit and Chloe watched the lacy curtain over the door's window swish as the door swung shut. She turned back to the Bennets. "Who are they?"

"Who is whom?" Charlotte waved a graceful hand in the air. "Oh, not them, dear girl." She, Betty and Jane Bennet exchanged a knowing look. "Your brother Jack and his Laurel."

Chloe glanced over to a table on the other side of the café, currently occupied by her brother and his wife of five months. Jack and Laurel still generated those sparks that she could clearly see, sparks that had flown between them even last year when they'd first met. She smiled at the memory of how hard they'd tried to keep their involvement a secret. Keeping that secret, or any secrets for that matter? Not a chance. Not here in the cozy little town of Cloud Canyon, anyway. "Oh, yeah."

The old ladies giggled and nodded almost in unison. They looked alike enough to be triplets, all slight of build, with heart-shaped faces topped by silvery fringes of hair. Most likely in their sixties, though they'd never admit it, they appeared quite sweet. But they could also be known to make the most ribald comments in their singsong, cultured voices. Chloe knew they never missed a trick, either. Or a chance to have the inside track on a juicy piece of gossip.

"Yes." Jane winked. "Big strong man, your brother."

"Sure," Chloe answered.

"Strapping," Betty said.

"Okay," she said.

"Makes me wish I was thirty years younger," Charlotte added. "Though I just bet I could give him a run for his money right now."

Chloe closed her eyes and let out a breath as she refrained from picturing Charlotte and her brother together. *Save me.*

Charlotte then gasped with an unnecessary amount of drama.

Chloe's eyes snapped open. "What?"

The elderly woman gestured toward the door. "Yes, Jack and that cousin Bo of yours. They sure are something."

The bell above the door jangled again as Bo Butler strode into the café. "Hey, cuz!"

Chloe rolled her eyes now and turned to Bo. "Hey, Bo."

"What's cookin'?"

"Ha ha." She ran her eyes over him, noting only a few smudges on his well-worn jeans and the navy T-shirt spanning his wide shoulders. "You're eating lunch here today?"

"Don't worry." He threw a wink in the direction of a table full of out-of-town women who almost purred in response. "I cleaned up real good."

Chloe shook her head. "This place is way too testosterone-y today."

The Bennets giggled again and murmured in agreement.

Her cousin Bo was a charmer, a hound dog through and through, and a lot like a guy she once fell for. Hard. Nick Stockton had the same killer charm up to his gorgeous crystal blue eyes, though she had no affection for him like she did for her family. He was nothing to her. Nothing except for a once-in-a-while dream, a healthy dose of regret, and just a touch of nostalgia. Nostalgia! That must be what's making her all fluttery today.

She nodded to the ladies and walked to the carved oak service counter. After setting the coffee pot back on the warmer, she ran her hands over the edges of the napkins stacked on the counter until they all lined up perfectly. She let out another breath. Nostalgia or not, why was she thinking about Nick today?

Nick, who had taught her naïve, twenty-year-old self that passion and love could be experienced simultaneously. Nick, who had stolen her heart in a blink. Nick, who had been out of her life for the past six years after all of seven amazing days in it.

Nick, who had the same tousled blond hair and heart-melting grin she saw every day in their son.

Breathing in deeply through her nose, she let the familiar scents of the café fill her head. The salt and butter smells of grilled sandwiches and French fries. The rich aromas of fresh coffee and cinnamon scones. And under all of it crisp lemon cleaner mingling with the unavoidable pine from the towering trees surrounding all of Cloud Canyon.

Home. She blew out the breath. *Hers.*

She gave the napkins one final pat and picked up a pitcher of iced tea. So what if she hadn't had any masculine attention since… When had Laurel set her up on that pitiful blind date? That was on Valentine's Day of all days! So about four months ago, although no stretch of the imagination could turn her evening with Ken the accountant into a romantic rendezvous. At least they'd only shared drinks in the lounge at the Treetop Inn and hadn't had to sit through a meal together.

So what if she didn't have any romance to speak of in her life? She had Cloud Canyon and the life she'd built here. She had her café and her family. She had her little boy, whom she loved with every bit of her. Every other day it was enough. Crossing to the table of out-of-town girls still drooling over her cousin Bo, she smiled and refilled their glasses.

What was so different about today?

***

Nick Stockton drove along US 80 toward the heart of the Sierra Nevada. He'd left Reno and Stockton Homes behind him for the time-being and embraced the first real assignment his father had ever given him. The rate of growth seemed to have flattened in Reno, so it was up to Nick to find a new direction for his father's company.

"West is as good a direction as any," he said to himself.

He punched the buttons on the radio, getting only static as the road climbed higher. Even the satellite was having issues, but he located a station with one of his favorites. "Springsteen. Why not?"

With the sound of the Boss blaring through the superior sound system of his new Ridgeline, he checked the dashboard clock. Twelve thirty-seven. He'd passed through Truckee about a half hour ago, and now he just saw more tall trees on either side and as much narrow road ahead of him as he saw in the rearview mirror. Then he spotted the sign for Cloud Canyon. Recognition niggled at the back of his mind. Cloud Canyon? Why was the name of that town so familiar? He hardly drove out this way, usually heading to Lake Tahoe whenever he strayed outside of Reno. Then it struck him.

"Chloe Butler." Her name on his lips did funny things to his head, as memories of the one that got away crystalized. "Damn."

He'd met Chloe in Reno during a builders' conference he'd attended with his father. Six years ago his job with Stockton wasn't much different than what it was now, though his current assignment was a stark exception.

She hadn't been one of the bored wives of his father's clients waiting to be amused, though. Or a tired cocktail waitress hoping to pass some time with a young guy with nothing but time on his hands. No, she'd been one of a group of college girls playing at sophistication, all of whom looked way out of place in the casino. He'd doubted that any of them had even been old enough to drink.

He'd known right away that Chloe was different, although he couldn't have imagined what they would mean to each other in the coming days. Sure she was gorgeous, with long brown hair and big eyes a shade of blue he'd never seen before. Sure she had a body he couldn't have dreamed up in all of his fantasies. But that week he'd spent with her, in and out of bed, had given Nick the hope that he could be more than a boy toy or a dumb kid jumping through hoops for his father. After the blowup when she'd left, though? He might have only been twenty-two but he'd known down to his soul that he would never get another chance with her or any woman like her. And that was just about six years ago.

Damn, has it been that long?

Nick glanced into the rearview mirror again. At

least the past six years had given a few rough edges to his pretty-boy face. It was a pity that his father still didn't think he was worth much more than that to the company. Joe Stockton never gave Nick anything more to do than schmooze the wives of the clients Stockton Homes was courting, despite his aptitude for design in addition to his MBA. Until this assignment, that was. And it had taken all of Nick's powers of persuasion to get it.

He approached the exit for Cloud Canyon and smiled. Chloe lived there, or at least she had back then. It was lunch time. And he should put more gas into the Ridgeline's tank. Why not stop in Cloud Canyon? There didn't seem to be any other town nearby. Pulling the wheel to the right, he took the exit.

As he drove through what seemed to be the center of town, he saw strips of stores and restaurants with façades that made them look like they were individual buildings. The place sort of resembled a colorful, down-sized version of Carson City. He would call it quaint if he had to sell someone on Cloud Canyon. Quaint with a rustic, Western style. He could almost see it on the glossy brochure, awash in sunset colors and maybe a horse or two.

There were plenty of cars parked near the clothing and antique stores, and a decided lack of hitching posts. "So, no horses, then."

He really wasn't surprised at the number of people strolling and shopping along the wide sidewalk, since Cloud Canyon was on the direct route toward Lake Tahoe. One store had stubby tree trunks carved into bears and moose for sale. Another had Native American art and the one next to that had thick sheepskin rugs done in browns and tans spilling over racks set on the sidewalk. Everything was arranged in an effort to attract.

"I bet the locals make a nice buck."

Then he saw a place called the Cloud Café, sandwiched between a clothing store and a hair and nail place in a stretch of several storefronts. "Breakfast and Lunch" was painted in white script letters across the wide front window framed with blue trim and dark red shutters. He pulled the truck into a spot two spaces down from the café and parked.

As he stepped into the café, a bell above the door jingled. The place was furnished with painted chairs and tables and had artsy pictures and metal advertising signs up on the walls. The sounds of cups on saucers and utensils on plates, along with conversations, filled the air. The smell of cinnamon was in the air too, along with strong coffee and what could only be French fries. His stomach growled. This could be good.

"Just sit anywhere," a brown-haired waitress said from the back of the restaurant. "I'll be right with you."

Most of the tables were occupied, but he saw an empty one set toward the back of the dining room and started toward it. Two young women got up to leave as he walked past their table, smiling as they eyed him up and down. He smiled back out of habit and kept walking.

The brunette who'd told him to sit stood behind a low counter. She had her back to him as she reached up to pour coffee grounds into the top of the machine. Nick sat down at his table and watched with appreciation at the khaki shorts hugging her butt. She had a long ponytail which swung to one side as she turned slightly. Hmm. Nice rack under that apron, too. She turned around fully and he felt a punch to the gut. He couldn't believe it was her. Chloe Butler. It was as if his memory had somehow managed to make her appear in real life. *Damn.*

She ran her hands over her apron and started toward his table. On second thought, it couldn't be his memory to blame. She was more beautiful than he remembered, and she wore the last six years very well. Her face, her body… Wow.

"Hi, what can I—?" She froze, those incredible blue-gray eyes of hers going round. Nick felt that punch again, along with a lick of desire.

"Hi, Chloe," he managed to say.

She blinked at him. "Nick," she breathed.

He took in a breath himself, slowly, and let it out. "Been a long time."

She shrugged, but the gesture appeared a little shaky. "Has it?"

Nick swallowed and leaned forward. "You work here?"

She stiffened a little. "This is my café."

He heard it in her voice then, that spark of spirit he'd noticed before but forgotten since. She'd been spunky and quick-witted, he now remembered. Their conversations had been nearly as stimulating as the rest of the stuff they'd done together back then.

He smiled and nodded. "Nice place. What do you recommend?"

She licked her lips and looked around the café, her gaze landing on a table toward the front window. Nick turned his head and saw what caught her eye. The big guy sitting at that table studied them in return, his dark brows drawn together. Shit, was he Chloe's boyfriend? The guy stared holes in Nick's chest and Nick swallowed.

Then a man at another table, just as big as the first guy, lifted his head and stared at Nick and Chloe with that same protective curiosity. The truth struck Nick in the next second. *Oh, man.* They both had eyes the same blue as Chloe's, that color he couldn't quite name. He hadn't realized that she had so much family, though she had talked about them back in Reno. She'd never mentioned just how big her family was though, physically speaking.

She faced him again, her expression shuttered now. "The patty melt is good."

Brr. The tone of her voice was downright chilly. Fine. He'd play it her way. It was her place, after all. Her town too, and her family looking on. At least the sandwich would be hot.

"Sounds good." He leaned back in the chair, letting his gaze touch every part of her. When he looked at her beautiful face again he watched her pupils dilate as her lips parted. Apparently she wasn't so cold, then. His throat went dry.

"And," he said as he glanced at the pitcher on the back counter and lifted his chin, "iced tea."

Chloe closed her mouth and turned, and he watched her. Mmm, she looked good as she walked stiffly back to the counter. Even freezing him out she was still the hottest thing he'd ever seen.

She returned with his glass of tea, set it down, and then left his table without another word. Maybe he should ask her to join him. To talk about, well, about anything but what had happened in Reno. Specifically, what had happened on that last morning in Reno. When she'd found him in bed with her friend and everything had blown up. He'd never even gotten the chance to... What? Apologize? Maybe if he got the chance to talk to her now he could at least set things straight. He'd been drunk and stupid, and even he didn't quite know which condition he'd been more in at the time.

The two big guys got up to leave, and Nick belatedly noticed the pretty blond woman with the first guy. She looked at Nick then Chloe, her head tilted to one side like she was trying to place him.

"Jack, who is that?" she asked.

"I don't know," the guy answered.

Whoa. If Chloe's tone had been chilly, this guy's could crush ice.

To Nick's surprise the woman grinned as she tugged the guy toward the door. "Interesting."

The couple left and the other big guy spared Nick another long look before looking at Chloe again. "See you tonight, Chloe?"

"Sure," Chloe answered.

Nick occupied himself with drinking his tea after the other Butler guy left the café. As he waited for his lunch, he watched Chloe buzz around the place. She was friendly with the customers, other than him that was, and they all seemed to respond to her. That was no surprise. When she smiled her whole body wore it. She was in her element, and her pride was evident too. He had to give her credit. Everyone seemed to be enjoying themselves, whether they were clearly acquainted with Chloe or apparently just passing through.

She dropped the plate holding a patty melt and fries in front of him and didn't linger for small talk. She didn't have any smiles for him, either. It was a good thing he was "just passing through" then, too.

Another waitress, a red-headed kid of about nineteen or twenty, refilled his iced tea. When Nick thanked her she stared for a long minute then sort of backed away, her brow furrowed over a curious stare.

As he ate what turned out to be a pretty great sandwich, he kept watching Chloe. He could see it, that spark he'd spotted earlier, in the tilt of her head and slight curve of her mouth even when she wasn't smiling. He could see it in the way she carried her body, that fresh sensuality that had caught his eye in Reno.

There had been something about Chloe Butler six years ago. There was still. Maybe he would stop by again later. He just couldn't make himself drive away from Cloud Canyon without another chance to see her. Was he being an idiot? Probably. Was he setting himself up for another cool reception? Most likely. Still, he would stop by again later.

He drank more of his iced tea.

To talk.

Chapter 2

"Who was that hottie?"

Chloe stacked the clean glasses behind the service counter. "What hottie?"

Jeanine laughed. "That guy who looks like Thor. I mean he's, like, old. But he's still a hottie."

Old? Chloe smiled at her. "He's just someone I used to know."

"Hmm." Jeanine took off her apron and left it on the counter. "He looks like somebody, though."

Chloe's heart skipped. "H-he does?"

"Yeah." Jeanine walked to the front door and turned. "I mean, other than the guy who plays Thor. See ya' in the morning."

"Okay." Chloe locked the front door after Jeanine left and pulled down the shades over the front window and the door.

Yeah, Nick looked like somebody. He looked like Josh.

Chloe's son. Nick's son.

She closed her eyes. Why was Nick here?

"You mean 'why can he still make you blush with

just a look?'" She pulled her apron over her head with a grunt. "I'm just romantically challenged, that's all. I don't want anything to do with him again." Been there, done that. Still had the T-shirt.

She went into the kitchen and dropped her and Jeanine's aprons into the bin to go to the laundry. Stepping back into the dining area, she took one final look around. The service counter and the area behind it was clean and tidy. The tables were spotless and set with clean napkins and utensils. The chairs were squarely set at each side of each table. The salt levels in the shakers could use some evening out, but she'd managed to stop running on that hamster wheel not long after opening the café. Everything was set for tomorrow's business.

Thank God her mother had kept Josh with her this afternoon. She could only imagine what a disaster it would have been if Nick had seen the little boy. Would he have guessed he was his? Maybe not, but she was sure glad he hadn't gotten the chance. It was bad enough that Jack, Bo and Laurel had been there to see her with Nick. Her family was nosy, to say the least. It wouldn't take much imagination for them to figure out who he was to her. And

Bo had the biggest mouth of all of them. He would spill it all over Cloud Canyon. She made a mental note to talk to Bo as soon as she could, then realized that would be tonight.

"Crap."

Tonight was the weekly dinner at her aunt's house. With the whole family. She knew Jack and Laurel had seen something. Even Bo, as dense as he was, sensed something between her and Nick. Double crap!

She took a deep breath. Nick had looked so good, though. Maybe he had some crinkles around those crystal blue eyes. Maybe his hair had darkened to a golden brown and he had some scruff on that jaw that used to feel so good when he rubbed it against her skin. When she'd stopped at his table that first time she caught his scent, fresh and warm and so Nick.

"Stop it, Chloe," she whispered.

When she'd seen him at the table, her heart had nearly stopped though. And later, when he'd run those gorgeous eyes over the front of her, she'd felt her body come alive for the first time in what felt like forever. It was like her hormones shook off the cobwebs and did a happy dance all over her common sense. Even now, her skin tingled as she pictured his well-formed mouth curved in that cocky grin.

A knock came at the door, two sharp raps.

"Jeanine?" Chloe unlocked the door and pulled it open. Oh, God help her. It wasn't Jeanine. Her breath left her in a rush. "You."

Nick leaned against the door jamb. "Hi, Chloe."

Oh, he looked as delicious as he had earlier, all tall and strong. Worn jeans hugged his narrow hips and long legs, and his white button-down shirt was just rumpled enough to drape softly from his broad shoulders. Chloe felt a rush of heat, as familiar as it was unwelcome.

She took a deep breath and found her voice at last. "What do you want, Nick?"

He shrugged, the movement smooth and practiced to her critical eye. "To talk, I guess."

"I don't—"

He smiled then, and any and all protests she might have made just fell out of her head.

"Can't we talk?" he asked. "Like old friends?"

She scoffed at that. However, she didn't want

anyone to notice him standing outside the café after closing time, least of all her aunt in the boutique next door or her mother just down the way at her antique store.

Nodding, she stepped back to let him into the café and then locked the door tight.

"Old friends, huh?" She faced him again, her hands placed squarely on her hips. "What do you want, Nick?"

"You look great, Chloe. Even better than before."

His practiced lines certainly helped her thoughts realign themselves and her nerves to settle. His voice was smooth, and deeper than it had been all those years ago. The years sure had been good to him, but she would cut out her tongue with one of Tom's sharpest knives before she would ever admit that to Nick.

"Yeah, right. Still the sweet-talker." She dropped her arms to her sides and walked toward the back of the café, eager to put some distance between them. "I really don't have time for this, Nick."

"Why? The place is empty. You're closed, right?"

She turned away from him and managed to keep from growling. How the hell would he know what her life was like? What she did after she closed for the day? Who took up her time and her heart every single day since she'd learned she was expecting him?

"I'm busy," was all the explanation she would give him.

She heard him step toward her. The air change around her, crackling with the same kind of sparks she'd seen between her brother and Laurel earlier.

"It looks to me like you have all the time in the world."

His breath tickled the tiny hairs on the back of her neck. He was close behind her. Way too close.

"I'm busy, Nick," she said again.

"Do you remember how it was, Chloe?" He leaned closer and she could smell him. Mmm, Nick. Fresh and warm and all male.

"Yes, I remember." She took a step away and turned to him, steeling herself against both the memory of back then and the reality of this particular moment. "I remember all of it."

"Me, too." A tilt of his head brought that tousled golden hair close enough to touch. "And I remember what you said, Chloe. What you told me right after our first time."

Oh, so did she. That night had been eye-opening for her. The taste of his lips against hers. The feel of his hands on her body. The rush of sensation and surrender.

"I'd just had my first orgasm, Nick. I can't be held responsible for whatever I said afterwards."

He grinned and brought his body a hairsbreadth away from her.

She placed her hand on his chest to gain more space. "I've had a few more since."

His lips thinned, and then he shrugged a shoulder. "Well, that was a long time ago. Six years?"

Almost to the day. "Just about."

Nick leaned against the counter behind him, his legs crossed at the ankles. His sleeves were rolled up and his forearms were tanned and strong. He looked way too comfortable in the place. *Her* place.

"Again." She placed one hand on her hip. "What do you want, Nick?"

"We never, um, got to talk about what happened in Reno. Earlier, I mean. You kind of froze me out."

So much had happened in Reno, both before and

after that horrible morning. Her cheeks flamed. "Yeah, so?"

"That was an amazing week, Chloe. *You* were amazing."

"Amazing is one way to put it." She shook her head to dispel the encroaching memories from clouding the senses over which she still had some control. "Humiliating is another."

He visibly sobered. "I admit the end of that week wasn't quite what I'd hoped for."

"No?" She welcomed the flare of anger when it came. "You didn't expect to get caught, huh?"

He straightened. "Look, Chloe—"

"No. You look, Nick. I've spent the last six years not thinking about that week in Reno. Not thinking about what I had foolishly believed we were to each other. Setting aside the dream of what we could be. That is, before I found you in bed with my best friend."

"Chloe, don't do this."

"Not thinking about what I'd felt for you, Nick." She jabbed him in the chest. "And not thinking about you at all."

"I don't think so." He grabbed her hand and tugged

her closer, stealing her breath. "Maybe that last morning was a horror show, but you can't deny that we shared something incredible."

She closed her eyes and tried to block out his touch as he stroked the inside of her wrist with his thumb. She struggled to hold on to her anger at his betrayal.

"Nick..."

He brought his lips to her ear. "That first night, Chloe." She could hear him breathe in as nuzzled her neck. "And the next night." He flicked his tongue over her skin, stroking down to her collar bone. "And the next..."

She looked at him from beneath her lashes. He eyed her with an expression she could only describe as hungry.

An answering heat flared within her and she stared at his mouth. It looked really tasty, that mouth. She stood on her toes and placed her lips on his. Nick groaned as she kissed him, letting her taste him for one long moment.

Then he crushed his mouth to hers, wrapping those strong arms around her until there was nothing but clothes between them. She tried to stop the kiss, but it was only one feeble motion soon buried under years of denial. Denial of what she'd felt for him then. Denial of what he apparently could still make her feel now.

When he grabbed her and pressed her against the counter, she gave up any semblance of resistance.

In one motion he reached up and freed her ponytail, stroking his nimble fingers through it. "God, Chloe." He kissed her throat, the skin just above the scooped neckline of her T-shirt. Oh, the feel of his lips against her skin!

Tugging his shirt out of his jeans, she ran her hands over his back. He was smoothly muscled. His skin was hot. Her fingers moved down and slipped just beneath his waistband, just brushing the curve of his butt. Oh, he felt so good.

He shrugged out of his shirt and she stared at him. He was gorgeous, sculpted and fit with just enough golden hairs to lead her eyes down his ridged belly.

She placed one hand on his chest, feeling the heartbeat that seemed in sync with hers. She wanted this. She wanted now. But she was in no position to indulge in anything so selfish and self-destructive as a romp with bad boy Nick Stockton.

He must have seen something in her eyes, though. Something that she couldn't hide or deny no matter how hard she tried.

"You want me." He sounded surprised.

"Yes." She squeezed her eyes shut. "Are you happy?"

He grabbed her and lifted her up onto the counter. "Not yet."

She heard the smile in his voice. When he leaned in closer she wanted to hold on and let go at the same time. A whisper of caution crept into her mind.

Her eyes snapped open. "Wait."

Nick froze and lifted his head to look at her. "Wait?"

She tried to catch her breath, and then the one question she could ask him popped into her head. His answer would tell her more than he would ever admit to right now.

"Do you have a condom?"

His eyes sparkled. "Yeah."

The cautious whisper became a shout, and she was almost disappointed that he'd proved her right. He was as big a hound dog as Bo. "Of course you do."

His brow furrowed for a moment, but she'd had a

flash of lifesaving clarity. She placed her hands on his chest again, holding him away from her. "No."

"Come on, Chloe."

Bewilderment cut through the desire she'd seen on his face and he suddenly looked years younger. And a lot like he'd looked in Reno.

That thought sobered her really fast.

"Nope."

He nodded and pulled away, easing her down off the counter. "This isn't why I came here."

She didn't say anything as she warily watched him. She used the moments he took to put on his shirt to regain her own composure. It wasn't easy, since her heart still raced and her body still tingled. At least her head was sort of in the right place.

"Listen." He stepped closer and she almost could feel him against her skin. "I came here to apologize."

"For what, Nick? For lying? For cheating?" *For hurting me more than anyone ever has, before or since?*

"For all of it, I guess."

"I don't want to hear it. Your words mean nothing to me. You mean nothing to me."

He stared at her for a long moment, his eyes sharp. "How can you say that? Are you kidding? I felt it in that kiss, Chloe. You can't deny that."

She finally summoned some courage, and raised her chin. "We had a fling, Nick. Years ago. It was nothing. This…" She waved a hand between them. "This was nothing."

His lips thinned again. "I want to talk to you, Chloe. See if we can be, I don't know. Maybe friends again. How about dinner?"

Dinner? As friends? No way. Even if a tiny part of her was tempted to go to dinner with him, she had to get home. She had to shower and change. She had to get Josh ready and get to her aunt's house for dinner.

"Thanks, but no," she said. "You have to go."

"I do? You sure about that?"

The question was there in his eyes, the offer to finish what they'd started. *Oh, yes.* No, no, no! She wanted to shove him out the door, but she feared that if she touched him she would lose any control she had left.

"Go, Nick."

"Fine." He nodded and shoved his shirttails into his

jeans. "I'll go. But this isn't over."

"*What* isn't over? Anything we had was over in Reno six years ago. Way over."

He walked to the door, then tilted his head toward the counter. "Keep telling yourself that." He unlocked the door. "Maybe you'll believe it."

She held on to her composure until he walked out of her life again. As the door closed behind him, she slammed her hand on the counter. "Damn him!"

***

Nick climbed into his truck and closed the door. He wrapped his fingers around the steering wheel and squeezed until he couldn't feel anything but the leather laces biting into his palms. He hadn't lied to Chloe. He really hadn't gone in there to have sex with her. But those kisses? Those had just happened. He was just a normal, red-blooded guy. He'd caught her sweet scent, felt the heat of her skin so close to his, and just couldn't help himself.

He rubbed his hands over his face. "Now who's lying?"

She was incredible. Hotter than any woman he'd had before her or after. And despite what she'd told him in no uncertain terms, he'd felt it again. That something more, that elusive thing that tickled the back of his mind during those seconds he'd held her in his arms. That amazing connection.

"You're wrong, Chloe." He jabbed the key into the ignition and turned. "This isn't over."

He pulled away from the curb and just started driving. Where he was going, he wasn't sure. But he wasn't leaving Cloud Canyon. Not yet. It was as good a place as any to use as his base of operations while he scouted locations for Stockton Homes. He glanced at the towering trees and the mountains in the distance everywhere he looked. You couldn't get better than summer in the mountains, right?

He saw a sign for an inn about two miles from Chloe's café and grinned. Maybe a couple of weeks spent near her would help him figure out what it was about her. Just what was it about this one woman that tied him up in knots?

He had to see her again. He pictured her as she'd been on that counter, pressed against him, her face soft with want. He could still taste her kisses.

Yeah, he had to see her again. Maybe he would be able to convince her to give him the sliver of chance to make things up to her. What happened after that, was anybody's guess.

Chapter 3

Chloe stepped out of the shower and scrubbed the towel over herself. It was no use. Her body still remembered Nick's touch. She wiped at the steam-fogged mirror with a corner of the towel and studied her face for a minute.

"You're a fool, Chloe Butler," she said softly. "Once more you were a convenient amusement for Nick-the-Playboy Stockton." At least this time she'd had the strength to stop him dead in his tracks. Not that it hadn't taken some doing on her part.

"Mommy?" Josh called from the other side of the door.

"What is it, Josh?"

"I gotta go."

"All right. Give me a minute?"

She heard him blow out a breath. "Okay."

"Okay." She blotted her hair dry and draped the towel over the bar set near the tub. "Almost done."

After slipping on her terry robe, she opened the door and stepped into the hall. Josh ran past her to the toilet and she closed the door. He had no sense of privacy, her son.

She heard the toilet flush. "Wash your hands."

"I know, Mommy."

"I know you know." When Josh came into her room she couldn't help but be reminded of Nick. The same hair, the same curve of his jaw. Thank God Josh's eyes were Butler-blue and not Nick's startling color. She knew she would have just about lost her composure if she looked into Nick's eyes right now.

"Get dressed, Mommy. I'm hungry."

"I'm sure Grandma gave you a snack this afternoon, Josh."

"Well, yeah. But Aunt Beth makes the best lemon squares."

"For after dinner." She turned him around and gently urged him out of the bedroom. "Out. Let me get dressed so we can go."

Dressed in a denim skirt and one of her sister-in-law Laurel's signature camisoles topped with a thin sweater, she felt more like herself at last. She combed her damp hair, slipped on a pair of sandals, and went out to the living room. Josh's hair was standing on end, again, when she found him glued to the TV. When she did the classic finger-lick smash down, he squirmed.

"Are you ready now, Mommy?"

She studied his face for a second, seeing Nick more clearly than ever. *This is Josh. This is my son.* "Yes, baby. Let's go."

Fifteen minutes later she parked her Wrangler in front of Aunt Beth's house. As they got out, Bo pulled up to the curb.

She rubbed her hand over Josh's back. "Go on in, honey."

"Hey, cuz!"

"Hey, Bo." She watched Josh until he went inside then faced her cousin. "What's up?"

"Not much. Who was that guy?"

"What guy?" It sure wasn't like any sort of evasion would put Bo Butler off the scent, but she couldn't help but give it a try.

"The guy at the café, Chloe. The pretty boy."

She kept her face blank. "He's no one."

Bo shook his head. "Yeah, right. And he didn't look at you like you were naked."

41

She shot a glance at the thankfully empty front porch. "Jeez, Bo."

"And you didn't look back at him like you wanted to be naked."

Chloe opened her mouth to tell him to shut up.

"Chloe?" her mother called from the porch. "What's keeping you?"

Chloe waved. "Be right there, Mom." After her mother closed the front door, Chloe glared at Bo. "Look, Bo. That guy is no one."

Bo pulled back, his brows raised. "Whoa."

"Just leave it alone." She ran a hand through her still-damp hair and sighed. "Please?"

"Okay." He turned and started up the walk. "No skin off my nose if you and some pretty boy do the—"

"Bo!"

He grinned over his shoulder as he stepped onto the porch.

Closing her eyes for a moment, Chloe took a breath. *Give me strength.*

Most of the Butlers were seated at the table when she walked into the dining room. Josh knelt on the chair next to Bo, and he was already chewing on a dinner roll.

Her brother Jack walked in from the kitchen, carrying in a platter of grilled chicken breast smelling of rosemary. He set it on the table. "Sis."

"Jack," Chloe said. "Sorry we're late, everybody."

Aunt Beth came out of the kitchen with a large wooden bowl of her famous greens-and-berries salad. "Just a little bit late, dear. No worries."

Jack sat beside Laurel. "So what kept you?"

"I…" Unable to withstand Jack's unwavering stare, she turned her attention to Laurel. "Hi, Laurel."

Laurel smiled, but her brows were raised in an expression of open curiosity. Chloe really wanted to get Laurel alone and bend her ear, even if it meant admitting all that Nick had been to her. Heck, who he still was to her if this afternoon was any indication. If anyone would understand, it was her sister-in-law and best friend.

Laurel and Jack had engaged in more than one secret rendezvous last year before they'd hooked up for good. But she couldn't talk to Laurel right now. Not with every Butler in Cloud Canyon watching her so closely.

Her mother put a piece of chicken on Josh's plate

and cut it up. "Sit down and relax, Chloe. You work too hard."

Bo snorted but Chloe chose to ignore it.

"Was the café busy, dear?" her aunt asked. "The boutique certainly was."

Her aunt owned the shopping strip that housed the café and also ran the clothing store next to it. The café, Chloe's mother's antique store and Laurel's nearby art studio and gallery finished what was rapidly becoming known as Butler's Bazaar.

"It's June," Laurel said. "Height of tourist season."

"Height of idiot season, you mean," Jack said. "Fools tramping through the Forest with no common sense."

"You love being a Ranger and you know it, cuz," Bo said. "So what if every once in a while you come across a couple of tourists doing the—"

"Bo!" Chloe said.

Bo reddened as he glanced at Josh. "Sorry."

"Doing what?" Josh asked.

"Nothing," Chloe answered for Bo. She sat down, watching Bo's mind work as he tried to backpedal out of the subject. Before he could even think to mention Nick again, she turned to Laurel. "Was the studio busy?"

"Oh, yeah." Laurel smiled. "A lot of the pieces I made in the winter are sold."

"No wonder," Chloe said. "Every time a customer asks about that stained-glass panel hanging up behind the counter, I send them over to you."

"That's the best advertisement," Aunt Beth said with a wink. "Maybe you should wear Laurel's tops while you work and send the customers over to the boutique."

In addition to her stained-glass studio, Laurel ran the designer clothing business her late mother had started. Original tie-dyed fabric and flirty designs made her tops hot sellers on the Internet and in Aunt Beth's store.

Chloe ran her fingers over the delicate crystal beads trimming the edge of her blue top. "I would love to but it wouldn't be practical."

"True." Laurel arched a brow. "But those colors look great on you."

"Thanks." The colors, shades of blue which picked up the crystal clarity of the faceted beads, reminded her of Nick's eyes. She swallowed a groan. *Way to put him out of your mind.*

"Besides, shouldn't you forget about being practical now and then?" Laurel added.

"I don't think so." Nope, that was way too dangerous. *Like this afternoon with Nick.* Those kisses hadn't been practical in the least.

Thankfully, talk soon turned to other topics, with everyone but Chloe contributing to the growing noise. Maybe later, when her son was tucked into bed and the house was still and quiet, she would allow herself the luxury of taking out today's memory of Nick and examining it. Savoring it. It had been a long time since she had anything like that to think about.

Thank God she'd stopped it at a few hot kisses.

***

That evening Nick walked up the street toward the Treetop Inn, not thinking about much else but Chloe and what they'd shared that afternoon. After he'd checked into the inn, he'd called his father to give him an update. Not about Chloe, of course. He and his father never talked about anything that personal. No, he'd informed Joe Stockton about his decision to base his operations in Cloud

Canyon for a couple of weeks. His father had seemed satisfied, and that was really as much as Nick could expect out of him. Joe never was one to gush over his one and only child, not when Nick was a kid and certainly not now.

Nick glanced up at the towering trees that surrounded the town and breathed in deep. The scent of the pines was pungent and invigorating. And the views were something. It was like he could see every star overhead. The sky that afternoon had been a blue he hadn't seen in Reno in a long time, and the sunset had taken his breath away.

He'd grabbed a bite at a diner not far from the inn, which closed up shop almost before he'd paid his check. He was pretty much on his own tonight, as it looked like the town rolled up the sidewalks early. The stores and restaurants could make a mint if they stayed open later, but maybe the locals thought the place would lose its charm if they did. He didn't see much in the way of nightlife either. No bars in the main part of town at least, except for the lounge at the inn. He wasn't of much mind to go exploring outside the city limits tonight, though.

The Treetop had clearly been a grand private home

at some point, Victorian in style and beautifully appointed. The lobby and lounge of the inn was decorated in what he could only describe as old-fashioned Western chic, with reds and golds, globe lamps and lots of fringe. It was like Miss Kitty's place from some old movie with cowpokes and shady ladies. His guest room had surprised him when he'd checked in that afternoon, though. With its roughly-carved bed and simple fabrics, it was just this side of rustic.

He toyed with the idea of grabbing a drink in the lounge tonight, but sitting at a bar alone wouldn't help him put Chloe out of his mind. Turning his attention to Stockton's next project should do it, though he didn't really have an idea yet as to where it could go.

Nick climbed the stairs to the room he'd been given. No amenity was absent, from the tiny bottles of shampoos and stuff set on the granite bathroom counter to the flat-panel TV hanging above the fireplace. It was rustic, but luxurious. His mind began to work, just as he'd hoped. Maybe that was what Stockton should think about creating in the new development? Homey and convenient, cozy and cutting edge. A study in contrasts.

Refined and wild, like Chloe Butler. He couldn't

seem to get her out of his mind and by this point he was tired of trying to. She was an intriguing combination of sweet and sexy. Yes she was classically pretty, but there was more to her. She had a wildness that spoke to the wildness in him. And a vulnerability too, like the kind he himself kept hidden deep down inside. Their connection had been instantaneous in Reno. It was clearly still there now. What happened, or almost happened, between them today was evidence of that.

He had to stop thinking about her, though. Yeah, their kiss had been surprising. And incredible. Her rejection wasn't something he wanted to experience again anytime soon. That was for sure. She was still pissed, and he supposed she had good reason. Would she ever let him apologize for ending up in bed with her friend? With a pounding headache and a wicked hangover on that last morning, he'd had no real idea how the hell he'd even gotten there. He sure didn't remember sleeping with what's-her-name.

He stripped and piled his clothes on the chair in front of the fireplace. "Yeah, Chloe Butler is a study in contrasts." He ran his fingers through his hair. "Hot and cold."

He walked into the bathroom. On closer inspection he noticed the large tub was jetted. Nice. He wasn't really a bath guy but maybe with the right company he could make good use of it.

He imagined Chloe in the tub. All smiling and rosy, her gorgeous hair wrapped around them as they splashed around. Another stab of desire hit him and he cursed softly.

"Like that'll happen any time soon," he muttered.

He stepped into the shower, turning the large chrome handle until the spray pounded on him.

Later, dried off and wearing nothing but a pair of sweatpants, he pulled his laptop out of his leather briefcase and set it on the desk. Pushing aside the lamp that appeared to be made of deer antlers, he opened the computer and pulled up the Stockton files. It was way too early to even try to sleep, so he opened a new file and started recording some ideas for Stockton's new direction.

Direction and a sketch of a study in contrasts.

***

The soft knock at the front door startled Chloe out of her solitude. Josh was long asleep and she sat in the kitchen drinking a cup of chamomile tea, trying to calm her nerves still jangling from seeing Nick today. The knock came again. Well, she knew who waited out there. No question.

She crossed to the door and pulled it open. "What took you so long?"

Laurel stood there with a grin, her eyes bright. "Good. You're up."

"Yep." Chloe closed the door and faced her. "How did you get away from my brother?"

Laurel winked. "Trust me, he'll be out of it for at least a couple of hours." She sat down at the table. "Well? Are you going to tell me who he is?"

Chloe sighed and sat across from her. "Can't you guess?"

Laurel sobered and nodded her head. "I suspected as much. He's the spit and image of Josh."

"Don't I know it. Jack didn't see it?"

Laurel shrugged. "I don't think so. But he knows something's up, Chloe. Heck, even Bo is suspicious."

Chloe rolled her eyes. "Why do I have to be a Butler?"

Laurel laughed softly. "Deal with it, babe. You have to take the bad with the good. So what are you going to do?"

Chloe looked away. "Nothing."

She could feel Laurel's close scrutiny and held herself still but she couldn't stop a flush from spreading over her face.

Laurel sucked in a breath. "You didn't!"

"How do you—? You scare me sometimes. Are you sure you didn't inherit some of your mother's intuition?"

Laurel smiled again.

"No, I didn't," Chloe went on. "But I almost did." She blew out a breath. "You're not going to tell Jack." It wasn't really a question.

"It's not my place."

Chloe buried her face in her hands. "I'm a colossal fool."

Laurel touched her arm. "No, you're not. You still feel a connection. It makes sense, Chloe. He's the father of your son."

Chloe shook her head and faced Laurel. "No, Laurel. He's the guy who got me pregnant. He has nothing to do with Josh. And he never will."

Laurel pursed her lips, then nodded. "Are you going to see him again?"

"God, no."

Laurel arched a brow. "Really?"

"Do you see him sticking around Cloud Canyon? It's not exactly his usual hangout."

"If you say so. You know him, not me."

"Yeah, I *knew* him, Laurel. A long time ago." Her eyes pricked, hot with tears. "At least I thought I did."

"He really screwed up, didn't he?"

Chloe swiped at her eyes. "No. I screwed up. Back then and again today. I don't know how I stopped myself, but I'm so grateful I did."

"You have a connection to him," Laurel said again as she stood. "That's a tough thing to deny. Call me if you need anything. Even if you just want to talk."

She knew Laurel was dying to know more. That she was itching to give Chloe advice and maybe let her pour her heart out. She also knew that Laurel would follow her lead. No matter what Chloe needed, she could expect to find it from Laurel. She was the perfect best friend.

Chloe stood and hugged her. "Thanks."

Laurel left her to her cold cup of tea and her warm memories of Nick. Nick then and Nick today. No matter what Laurel had said, Chloe knew she was a fool.

And a tiny part of her wanted to be foolish again.

***

When Nick woke the next morning, it was with the familiar sense of the unfamiliar. He spent lots of nights in hotels on Stockton business and was used to waking up alone. But this morning it bothered him. The bed was wide and comfortable, with sheets that were probably Egyptian cotton, but he had no desire to lay around in it. Not alone.

He shaved, dressed and went down to the lobby. Nodding a greeting to the old guy at the front desk, he went over to the display rack of brochures advertising the sights to see in and around the area.

"Casino excursions?" Nick flicked his finger over one glossy brochure declaring the fun, fun, fun to be had in Reno just a short bus ride away. "Been there, done that." He dismissed the ads for Lake Tahoe just as quickly.

"Lookin' for a way to spend your day, young fella?"

Nick turned to the guy at the front desk. "Sort of."

The gray-haired man looked to be somewhere in his sixties and his pale blue eyes sparkled behind wire-rimmed glasses. "Working trip, then?"

"Yes." Nick crossed to the desk. "Do you get a lot of business travelers in Cloud Canyon?"

"Some. Usually just passing through, though." He folded his hands on the leather blotter. "Not much business around here. Mostly recreation. So what are you doin' here?"

"Just checking out the area."

"Never been here before?"

Nick shook his head. "It's nice, though."

"Yep, it is. Lived here all my life." He held out his hand. "Fred Bennet."

Nick shook his hand. "Nick Stockton."

Fred Bennet gave his hand a firm shake and released it. "Well, Nick Stockton, what are you looking for?"

Nick thought for a moment. Contrasts. A place for Stockton to establish a brand that would draw people looking for escape yet would still have all the modern conveniences. State-of-the-art, he could do. The company was built on that. But escape? Back to nature? There, he needed a whole lot of help.

"Actually I'd like to get a feel for the place. For the natural aspects of the area. The open spaces, I guess."

Fred Bennet nodded. "You'll want to hit the Forest then."

"The Forest?"

"The National Forest, son. Tahoe National Forest, to be exact. Lots of scenery to soak up."

"Sounds good. Do I need a pass or anything?"

"Here." Fred stepped out from behind the desk and crossed to the brochure stand and withdrew a flyer. "This lays out the trails and recreation areas. You can pay at the guardhouses of any of the marked locations."

"Thanks." He turned to go, then stopped as he thought of something. "Is there any place I can grab breakfast?"

"The Cloud Café," Fred answered. "Chloe Butler serves up a killer breakfast."

Nick kept his expression blank. "Yeah. Um, any place else?"

Fred blinked. "I suppose the diner is passable. Just

head south through town."

The diner from last night. Passable was a good way to put it.

"Anywhere else?"

Fred shrugged. "There's a bakery not far from there."

"Thanks again."

"My pleasure. Have a good day."

Nick nodded and stepped out of the inn. He climbed into the truck, tossed the National Forest brochure on the seat next to him, and drove down to the bakery. After grabbing a quick cup of coffee and a bear claw, he consulted the map Fred Bennet had given him.

"Okay. Looks like Soda Springs is the closest recreation area." He started the truck again and headed in the direction the map indicated. "Sounds...bubbly."

Nick found the turn-off easily enough and followed the signs to the rec area. Gravel crunched beneath the Ridgeline's tires as he made his way down to what he guessed was the guardhouse. There was a skinny kid leaning out the window of the little wooden building, eyeing the teens in the car in front of Nick's as he waited for their passes or whatever. When Nick pulled to a stop beside the guardhouse in his turn, he opened his window.

"Good morning."

"Welcome to Soda Springs," the kid said. "Do you have a pass for the Forest?"

"Not yet. What do I need?"

"Well, you can buy a pass for today or multi-day. Or more." He ran down the prices.

Nick thought for a moment. The Forest was huge, and probably filled with plenty of places to get his inspiration. "I'll take a multi-day to start." He fished out his card and paid him.

"Thanks." He handed Nick his pass. "Have a great day."

Nick nodded and drove down a curving road toward the crowded parking lot. He parked the truck and watched the people wading and fishing in the water or lounging on the rugged bank. The place was pretty crowded despite the early hour, which told him recreation meant something a little bit different here in the Forest than it did over in Reno or even Lake Tahoe. Good. He took that as an encouraging sign. More hours of activity meant more to do and see, which might just mean more people interested in the new ideas Nick was busy formulating.

He got out of the truck and as he walked down to the water he spotted a man dressed in a green Forest Ranger uniform. He turned and Nick was struck with recognition. It was one of the big guys from Chloe's café yesterday. The one who'd been with the pretty blonde, and had stared him down. Hard.

Squaring his shoulders, Nick stepped toward him. "Hello."

"Good morning." His voice was chilly this morning, too.

The guy eyed him for a long moment from under the wide brim of his Ranger hat and Nick's gaze fell to his name badge. *Butler.*

Nick swallowed. "You're Chloe Butler's...?"

"Brother. Jack Butler." Those blue-gray eyes regarded him again. "Who are you?"

"Nick." He held out his hand. "Nick Stockton."

After a flicker of hesitation, Jack Butler shook his hand. "How do you know Chloe?"

Nick waited a beat as he quickly considered how he

should answer. In the biblical sense? Somehow he didn't think this guy would appreciate the joke.

"I knew her a long time ago."

The guy's eyes narrowed. "When?"

When? That was an odd question. How about "how well?" or "from where?"

"About six years ago," Nick said at last.

His eyes widened in obvious surprise. His gaze searched Nick's face for what? Nick couldn't guess.

In the next instant Jack's expression grew shuttered. "Why are you here?"

"Here?" In Cloud Canyon or in the National Forest? Nick wasn't going to press Chloe's brother for clarification.

"My company's considering building in the area," he answered. "I need to get a feel for the surroundings."

Jack Butler arched one dark brow. "Building what?"

"Homes." Nick glanced at the scenery behind Jack Butler and something struck him. "Cabins."

Nick hadn't really thought about the structures, but it suddenly made sense. Luxury cabins, actually. If such a thing could be accomplished, he'd sure as hell figure out a way.

Chloe's brother gave a curt nod. "Where are you thinking of building?"

Nick shook his head. "Not sure yet. I need to find out what land's available. Do you know a good realtor?"

He shrugged. "Maybe. I think I have her card." He pulled out his wallet and thumbed through the papers tucked inside. "She's always pushing them on me whenever I run into her in town. Here."

As Nick took the card from Jack, a snapshot in one clear plastic sleeve of his wallet caught his eye. He stuck the card in his pocket as he continued to stare at the photo. A little boy who looked about five years old smiled at the camera, his blond hair sticking up as he laughed at whoever took his picture.

There was something familiar about the boy, something about the eyes of that same blue-gray as every Butler he'd ever met. But there was something else, too.

"Is that your son?" Nick asked.

"Shit," Jack muttered. He flipped the wallet closed, his lips thinned to a line as he shoved it into his back pocket. "No. That's my nephew. Josh."

Nephew? Nick's heart pounded as his stomach

clenched tight. *OhGodOhGodOhGod*. "Your nephew?"

"Yeah." Jack let out a breath. "Chloe's son."

Chapter 4

Chloe set the iced tea pitcher on the service counter and eyed Jack and Laurel where they sat. Their heads were close together but they weren't engaged in their usual billing and cooing. No. Laurel looked upset and Jack's scowl was as dark as she'd ever seen it. They hardly ever argued, so what the heck was going on?

When Laurel's troubled gaze settled on her, Chloe's heart dropped. Whatever it was, it had to do with her. This couldn't be good. She knew that Laurel wouldn't tell Jack what they'd talked about last night but she knew in her heart that something was definitely up.

She crossed to their table and they both straightened and looked up at her. "Okay, spill. What's wrong?"

They exchanged a look that made the little hairs on the back of her neck tingle. Jack rubbed a hand over his face, apparently unable to look her in the eye now. That was a sure sign her brother felt guilty about something. *Uh oh.*

"What is it?" she asked.

"Tell her, Jack," Laurel said softly.

Jack blew out a breath and faced her again. "He

knows."

Chloe swallowed, her throat thick. "*Who* knows?"

"The pretty boy," he grumbled.

Her heart skittered to a stop. *Nick.* "Knows what?"

Jack lifted his head to meet her gaze. "He knows about Josh."

"Oh, no." She grabbed on to the edge of the table as the breath whooshed out of her. "How, Jack? How did he find out?"

"He saw Josh's picture in my wallet."

"What?" She blinked at him. "How the heck did he see your wallet?"

"His company's thinking about building around here and he asked if I knew a realtor. When I was handing him Krissy's card, he saw Josh's picture."

"Krissy?" Chloe straightened. "Once again Krissy manages to eff up my life."

Laurel gave her a small smile. "I don't think you can pin this one on Krissy."

"I'm so sorry, sis."

Regret was so clear on Jack's face that she couldn't really be angry.

"How did he react?" Chloe couldn't help but ask.

"He turned whiter than… well, I've never seen anyone turn that white."

Chloe's mind worked as her heartbeat slowly returned to normal. Nick knew about Josh. Maybe this wasn't that bad. Maybe this solved the problem of how to deal with her weakness for the only guy she'd ever loved. If she knew anything about Nick, she suspected that he wouldn't stick around Cloud Canyon once he knew about her little secret. He and his heart-melting smile would get out of town in a big hurry.

"Well," she said. "If I wanted Nick Stockton to leave Cloud Canyon I couldn't think of a quicker way."

Jack's brows drew together. "If?"

Chloe just shook her head and turned away from their table, her stomach in a tight knot. The Bennet sisters' gazes followed her as she walked toward the service counter, sharp interest lighting their eyes. Imagine if they found out about Nick and Josh? The news would be all over town before sunset.

It really didn't matter who found out what or how. Nick was probably on his way out of Cloud Canyon at this very moment, happy for his narrow escape. Good. If he was gone for good, she would never have to worry about seeing him again.

That's just what she wanted, wasn't it? Yet that foolish spark of hope still burned inside her. That darn dream she just couldn't shake. The dream that Nick could be a real father to Josh.

"Yeah, right," she murmured. "That will never happen."

***

Nick stood in front of the café around four that afternoon. He wiped his sweating palms on his jeans, then rubbed his hands over his face. That picture was burned into his brain, the image of the son he never knew he had. The kid's big eyes, that easy grin. There was no mistaking the Stockton chin. His son was a looker.

His first instinct was to get the hell out of Dodge, and when he'd escaped Jack Butler and climbed into the truck he was set to do just that. The urge had burned in his gut to turn back towards Reno and forget everything about Cloud Canyon. About Chloe. And about Josh. But he couldn't do it. Instead he'd left the National Forest and just driven around the area, his mind a swirling mess. Then he'd headed to the Cloud Café. He had to talk to Chloe. That was for sure.

He had a lot questions. Why hadn't she told him she was pregnant back then? What about after Josh was born? How the hell could she keep this secret for six years? And there was one question he was itching to ask more than any of the others. What was their son like?

"Yep," he said as he parked in front of the café and switched off the ignition. "Those questions will do for a start."

He got out of the truck and walked up to the café door. After he took in a breath, he rapped on the window. One long minute passed before the curtain behind the glass twitched. When he heard the latch click he let out the breath he'd been holding.

Chloe opened the door, her expression flat. "Hello, Nick."

He stepped into the café and let her lock the door behind him. Just like she'd done yesterday. His goal today was far different than yesterday's, though.

"Why didn't you tell me?" he asked.

"Nick—"

"I had a right to know."

Her eyes went round. "No. You threw away any rights that morning when I caught you in bed with Krissy."

Nick winced at the reminder. That terrible morning in Reno had turned out to be the defining moment of his life, up until learning about his son today. Chloe had found him tangled in the sheets with her friend, but his memory was still hazy on the circumstances. He sure didn't remember sleeping with her, either.

"You still should have told me."

"I didn't know how to get in touch with you. I tried to find you on one of the social networks and when I couldn't I sent a message to Stockton Homes."

He thought for a second. "I'm not surprised I never got it, then. The company wasn't exactly tech savvy back then. I'm not even sure who monitors Stockton's inbox."

"I sure didn't have your number."

That he knew was true, and he didn't have hers either. He hadn't thought to exchange info since he'd never plan to let her go back then.

"I… When can I see him?"

"You won't see him." She turned away and took a few steps away from him. "Not ever."

His chest tightened, with hurt or anger he wouldn't guess at this second. "Chloe, this isn't right."

She whirled to face him. "I'm his mother and I decide what's right. I won't let him get hurt."

That stopped him for a moment. Like he'd hurt her? Yeah, that made a kind of horrible sense.

"I'm so damn sorry about Reno." Nick took a breath and slowly let it out. "But do you honestly think I would hurt our kid?"

"Oh, Nick." She slowly shook her head. "You wouldn't even have to try. Josh would get to know you, maybe even to count on you, and then you would just… disappear."

"Maybe not." Guilt pulled at him, though. Hadn't he thought about doing just that this morning? But he'd come here instead, hadn't he? "Give me a chance, Chloe."

"No. No." Her eyes glistened with tears and she trembled as she crossed her arms. "I can't let you see him. No!"

Nick wrapped her in his arms and she cuddled

against him for one sweet moment, her fisted hands between them as she shivered. He rubbed his hands over her back. He wanted to take her pain away. To ease her fears that he was as big a jerk as she thought he was. To make her see that he wasn't the same self-absorbed kid he'd been back then.

"Shh." He dropped a kiss on her hair. "All right." He cupped her face and brushed away her tears with his thumbs as he stared into her remarkable eyes. "All right. Let's put a pin in this and discuss it later."

She stiffened and he released her, his arms hanging empty now at his sides.

"No." She stepped away from him, her cheeks flushed. "God, no. No pin. No discussion later."

She pulled out the closest chair and sat down as though her legs couldn't support her any longer. He shoved his hands into his front pockets and watched her as she visibly collected herself. The vulnerable woman he'd just comforted was long gone. The wall was back up, and apparently it was as thick and impenetrable as ever.

After about a minute she scrubbed her hands over her cheeks and faced him with dry eyes. Her brow was smooth but he could still see worry lines around her mouth. "My brother said you're going to build here?"

Nick took a few seconds to recover from the swift change of subject, then pulled out the chair beside her and sat. "I think so. I have to scout the area and see if it will work for us."

"What are you thinking of building?"

"Cabins." Where was she going with this? He folded his arms and rested them on the table. "I'm just starting to work out the details."

She nodded, her brows drawn. "And how long will you be here?"

He began to grasp what she was thinking now. "At least a couple of weeks."

She stared at him, her gorgeous eyes narrowed slightly. "You can't see Josh."

Why did he feel that whatever he did now, at this moment, was very important? He gave her a slow nod and came to his feet. "It's your call."

Her relief was palpable as she relaxed her shoulders. Suddenly she jumped up and wrapped her arms around his neck. "Oh, thank you."

Her voice was breathy and soft and made him think all sorts of things. "God, Chloe." Nuzzling her neck, he breathed in her scent. "Mmm."

"Nick…"

She pulled back to stare up at him. *Those eyes*. No. He had to be imagining what he saw there. Unable to resist, he brought his lips to hers. The kiss was hotter than yesterday's, and just as sweet. He was tangled up in her, and he was seized with the desire to never let her go. Her curves pressed against him, and he cupped her butt and pulled her tighter still. He kissed her throat, and then the fragrant hollow just below.

"Nick," she sighed. "Oh, no one has ever made me feel this way."

He wouldn't let out a shout of victory at her admission. No. He wouldn't high-five himself or do anything but hold her in his arms right now. "Chloe, I can't…God, I want to finish what we started here yesterday."

Nick swallowed as he froze at what he'd just said. She would run from him now. He just knew it. He'd gone too far and she would pull away from him again. Maybe for good this time.

"I do, too." Her voice was breathy and soft, but he'd heard her agreement.

Man, that was all he'd thought about since setting foot in Cloud Canyon, up until learning about their son. He eased away from her, running his gaze over her flushed cheeks and rosy lips. "You do?"

She nodded. "Yes. But I have a proposition for you."

Her voice held a promise he never thought he'd hear from her again. *Easy, Nick.*

"What kind of proposition?"

She looked at him through her lashes. "Can't you guess?"

His blood pounded low and deep. "I can hope."

A smile curved her beautiful mouth now. "I survived a week in Reno with you."

"Yeah." And what a week it had been, until the end of it. "You did."

"Do you think you can survive two weeks in Cloud Canyon with me?"

"Yeah. I do." He moved his hands to settle on her

waist. "Survive or die trying."

He went to kiss her and she pulled back. "But it would be just this. Nothing else."

When he nodded his agreement her mouth settled on his again. He wouldn't think about her conditions regarding their son. He would just take what she offered him right now and deal with the rest of it later.

They would talk about their son, though. Before he left Cloud Canyon, they would have that discussion. He would apologize again for breaking her heart all those years ago, too. Later.

He started to lift her shirt, to stroke her breasts that fit his hands perfectly.

"Wait," she gasped.

He took a breath. "What?"

"We can't have sex in the café."

He smiled. "But I have a soft spot for that service counter. It's just the right height for—"

"Never mind." She pulled away, taking one of his hands in hers. "Come on."

She tugged him toward the back of the café.

"The kitchen? Chloe Butler has gotten kinky."

"Hardly. Come on upstairs."

He followed her up a narrow staircase behind the kitchen to stop in front of a closed door. She reached up and grabbed a key from on top of the door jamb and winked at him over her shoulder.

"What is this place?"

She opened the door and ushered him into a tiny living room. "My apartment." She put the key back and shut the door. "Well, it used to be. No one lives here now."

The living room had a couch and one chair and he could see a small kitchen through an archway. "You used to live here?"

"Before Josh was born."

She stilled as if she was back in that memory, one he hadn't been given the chance to share, and then gave a small shake of her head.

She led him into a cozy little bedroom beyond the kitchen and backed him toward the quilted bed.

"Are you sure about this?"

"Yes." She pushed him back onto the bed. "It might be the dumbest thing I've done in forever, but I'm sure."

He kicked off his shoes and leaned up on his

elbows, staring as she lifted her T-shirt over her head. Her breasts were full and round, just begging for his attention through her pink lace bra.

She reached up behind her and stopped, curving a smile at him. "Aren't you going to get naked?"

He sat up and undid two buttons of his shirt before pulling it up over his head. She dropped her bra to the floor and his mouth went dry. *Damn.*

He shifted on the bed until his back rested against the iron headboard. She knelt on the bed and touched him, running her hands over his chest. "Mmm, nice."

Her touch was soft yet left a trail of fire behind it.

She reached across him and pulled open the drawer in the nightstand. Her eyes shining, she held up a wrapped condom. "I was hoping I'd find one here."

She slid it over him and followed it down, taking all of him.

Nick squeezed his eyes shut as she began to move. He reached up to grab the head rail as she held on to his shoulders. He could feel every inch of her, moving faster and faster until his moans mixed with hers. He'd never felt anything so amazing. The incredible memories of their nights together in Reno faded as he felt more than he ever had before. She cried out in release and he shuddered as his climax struck him, shouting her name.

Afterward she collapsed against his chest, her breath tickling his skin as he tried to catch his own. Thank God they were on the bed. He could hardly move.

He shifted down and cradled her against his side, his heart slowing. "I won't ask how old that condom was."

"Not very."

Did she have other guys up here? Was this some kind of love nest? Well, he hadn't been celibate for the last six years. For the last six months, maybe. She was entitled to drag guys up here once in a while. He wouldn't think about that. Not while he held her. He was here with her now. Nick Stockton, not some faceless Cloud Canyon guy.

"My sister-in-law Laurel stayed here last year. When she and Jack first got together."

Relief flooded him. No mention of another lover, then. Good. Not that it should matter. But this was more than what he remembered from Reno, and not just the sex. It was that connection he'd never felt with another woman.

He turned and brushed a hair out of her face. "That

was amazing, Chloe."

"Yeah, it was," she breathed.

It felt right holding her like this, with her all soft and vulnerable like she'd been downstairs. Scents reached him. Her skin, her hair. He took in a deep breath. She smelled like flowers and cinnamon.

"I have to get home," she said.

Nick bit his tongue down on any argument. "Sure."

They separated and he ignored the chill that danced across his skin. He got dressed as she did the same, and then followed her out of the room. Once out in the hall, he touched her arm as she locked the door. "Chloe—"

"Just this, Nick. No apologies, no talk of seeing Josh." She looked up at him, her skin still flushed pink, and he wanted her again. "Can you do that?"

He would be a fool to turn down her offer. No-strings sex with the hottest women he'd ever known? "Sure." He could just take it as it came. "No worries."

She leaned up to kiss him and, for a brief moment, he tasted the promise of more.

Chapter 5

The next morning, Nick shifted on the bed and groaned softly. His cell phone trilled on the nightstand, letting him know what had woken him.

"Yeah, yeah," he mumbled, rubbing a hand over his face. He grabbed the phone and peered at the screen through one eye. Caller ID showed him it was his father on the line.

"Hi, Dad."

"Still in bed?" His father chuckled low in his throat. "Do you have company?"

Yeah, because Joe liked to live vicariously through Nick's conquests over the years. He'd teased him during his recent dry spell but Nick hadn't been able to admit just what it was that had turned him off of meaningless sex. Those damn memories of Reno with Chloe, even before he ever thought he would see her again. Now that he'd reconnected with her? There was no way he would share that with the old man.

Nick scratched his bare belly. "Nope. Just me. What's up?"

"What have you found?"

Should he tell his father about his son? About Josh? It was still too fresh for Nick to absorb. He couldn't guess how his father would react to instantly having a grandson. And with Chloe determined to keep Nick away from Josh, he didn't want to mention the boy when he had no idea if his parents would ever get the chance to see him.

"Well, I went into the Forest yesterday and the area is pretty amazing."

"The forest? Who are you, Goldilocks?"

Nick laughed and put his feet on the floor. "The Tahoe National Forest. I've got some ideas for the new direction of Stockton."

"Really? What are they?"

Nick heard the interest in his father's voice and it sounded genuine. Looking into the mirror set above the dresser, he brushed his hair back from his face. "It's just a couple of ideas, Dad. Something that should prove highly profitable if we can pull it off."

"Do you have anything to send me?"

"Not yet. I'm calling a realtor today and should hopefully get a handle on land availability soon."

Joe Stockton was quiet, and Nick knew the man's

mind was working furiously. Numbers and prospectus, materials and delivery. Stockton Homes had a network of preferred suppliers and financiers, and Nick knew that before the project got past the embryonic stage Joe would have to give Nick the green light.

He'd had lots of time to think on his drive from Reno yesterday, and had come to a decision. Either his father gave him the reins on this deal or he was out of it. Maybe out of Stockton Homes, should it come to that. His mother would wail and lament his desertion but Joe would most likely just take it stride and move on to his number two.

"Go to it, then," Joe said. "Keep me informed."

Nick held the phone away from his ear and stared at it for a moment. *Whoa.* He brought it back to his ear. "I will, Dad. Give Mom my love."

"Will do. Take care, son."

"Yeah. You, too."

Nick set his phone down on the dresser. "Well, I'll be damned." He walked toward the bathroom, his gaze falling on the rumpled sheets. Of course his father would think Nick would have some woman in bed with him.

Wasn't that his reputation? Though ever-faithful to Nick's mother, he never had any problems with Nick's tomcatting around. Make the clients' wives and daughters happy and the deals would follow. Wasn't that all Joe Stockton expected from him?

"Maybe." Nick thought about the small vote of confidence he'd gotten this morning. "Maybe not."

Today his father had listened to him. Really listened. He'd given Nick the chance to prove that the man could expect more from him. Nick would stay in Cloud Canyon and try to make his luxury cabin idea work. And doing so would give him more time with Chloe.

Chloe. She'd stunned him yesterday, with her proposition and her passion. He had to pay to play, though. She didn't want him to have anything to do with their son and he was in no position to defy her right now.

It was a shame that he couldn't mentioned Josh to his father. His mother would be over the moon to learn they had a grandson. But Chloe was determined to keep the kid away from Nick, and if he couldn't change her mind over the next couple of weeks he didn't stand a chance of having the boy in his life after whatever this was with Chloe was over.

Nick dropped his boxers and got into the shower, letting the water cool after he'd washed. He was tempted to forget about the realtor. To focus on nothing more than seeing Chloe at the café and getting her back in bed. The little bed in that apartment, his big bed here at the inn. He didn't care where. Just when, and soon.

His father was waiting for a report, though. Patiently, which still blew Nick's mind. If he could get some info and give his father an update in a day or two, all the better.

After he dressed in chinos and an oxford shirt, he went through his jeans pocket and fished out the card Chloe's brother had given him. The company was called Mountain Realty. The name of the realtor meant nothing to him, K. L. Bates, but the picture struck a faint chord of familiarity.

The photo on the card was an example of what was rapidly becoming the standard for realtors. It featured a flashy glamour shot to convince you that this pretty person had the skills to find you the property you wanted or to take the sale of your house into their manicured hands. The woman on this card looked polished and easy at the same time. He'd seen her type before. It did nothing for him. Chloe Butler, though. Clean and fresh, hot and wild. Chloe sure wasn't easy, but she was just his type.

If Jack Butler recommended this realtor, Nick should give her a shot. This woman looked like she schmoozed everyone in the area. No doubt she would know what properties were available at the best deals.

Nick sat on the edge of the bed and tapped the number on the card into his cell.

***

Chloe hummed to herself as she readied for the morning rush. She'd surprised the heck out of herself yesterday afternoon. She supposed she could blame at least part of it on her jangled emotions. After Nick had agreed to let her decide whether or not he could see Josh, she'd been overwhelmed with relief and gratitude. She'd wrapped herself around him, and oh! The smell of him. The feel of his arms around her. She'd been unable to resist her own desires in that second, so she'd jumped in with both feet.

Today she felt energized and alive. It had to do with the fact that she'd consciously made the decision to have sex with Nick on her terms yesterday. And he'd agreed to them. She couldn't let him see Josh. Not right now. But she couldn't deny that Nick was her only chance at any kind of passion in the foreseeable future. She could keep her heart out of it this time. She wasn't that same naïve girl she'd been in Reno. It didn't matter that it would only be for a couple of weeks. That made it all the better, actually. She was older and wiser now, and she could certainly survive two weeks of Nick before going back to her regularly-scheduled programming so to speak.

She wouldn't think about what had happened after the mind-blowing sex. Nope. She wouldn't think about the comfort she'd felt there in his arms. How right it felt to be held by him, his lips brushing over her hair as if he actually gave a crap about her. *Her*, Not Krissy. Not some other woman from Reno or Cloud Canyon or wherever he might have roamed over the past six years. She'd made that mistake once, though. She knew better now. Nick wasn't made for long-term, and that was just fine right now.

"Morning," Jeanine called from the kitchen, her voice a little breathless.

Chloe faced her employee as she hurried into the

dining area. "Good morning."

Jeanine grabbed a clean apron off one of the hooks near the kitchen and draped it over her neck. "Sorry I'm late. The cat got stuck under the dryer."

Chloe chuckled. "As excuses go, that's certainly original."

"Well, she was trying to get a sock…"

"It's okay, Jeanine. You're not so very late."

Jeanine stopped talking and tilted her head to one side to stare at her. Chloe could guess what she was thinking. She ran the café like she did everything, with attention to detail and no room for fudging. She wasn't a mean boss, just very rigid.

"Are you okay?" Jeanine asked.

"Fine." Chloe waved a hand at her. "Why don't you unlock the door?"

Jeanine nodded and crossed to the front of the café. Chloe ran her hands over her own apron to smooth any wrinkles and waited for the first of the morning's customers. The Bennet sisters were in the first wave of customers as usual. Each of them eyed her closely like Jeanine had done, putting their heads together and whispering none too quietly as they settled at their usual table.

"Oh, Chloe dear," Charlotte Bennet called when they had nearly finished their breakfasts.

Chloe took a breath and walked over to their table. "Good morning, ladies. I take it your meals were satisfactory?"

"Of course," Jane said. "Tom knows just how to make my egg-white omelet."

She waved to Jeanine who was circulating through the dining area with the coffee pot before facing the ladies again. "Did you need refills?"

"I wouldn't say no," Betty said. "Although I prefer to have whatever you had."

Chloe schooled her expression. "How do you mean?"

"You're positively glowing this morning, dear," Charlotte said. "Your eyes are bright. Your cheeks are rosy. I don't think mere coffee put that spring in your step."

"It's not just coffee." *No, I grabbed the hottest guy I know and did him upstairs like the world was ending.* "The chocolate chip muffins from the bakery are so good today."

"Mmm, yes," Betty said. "I've sampled those before. Positively sinful."

Chloe smiled brightly. "Yes."

Jeanine came over with the coffee pot. "More coffee, ladies?" The three sisters nodded in unison and she filled their cups.

"Jeanine, please bring them a couple of those chocolate chip muffins?" Chloe asked.

"Ooh, will do."

"Thank you, dear," Jane said before Jeanine left the table. "Now, Chloe. What aren't you telling us?"

She put a hand on her hip. "Oh, I make a point of never telling the three of you anything."

The ladies laughed out loud.

"Our girl is keeping secrets," Charlotte said. "At long last!"

Chloe refrained from rolling her eyes and shushing them. "I have no secrets. I've told you that before."

"Hmm, we'll see," Betty put in.

Chloe shook her head and made her way back to the service counter. Nick had wanted to do it right there, and she'd almost been tempted to for one hot second. That man could make her throw all of her good sense out the front picture window with one wink of those crystal-blue eyes. She would never let him convince her to change her mind about Josh, though. God help him if he tried. She had to work this through on her own, and in her own time.

By the time the morning rush was over, she was ready to scream. With every jingle of the bell above the door she'd expected Nick to walk in. She didn't want to see him right now. She suspected he would sport a smug expression, and she also knew she might not be able to keep from slapping off of his face. That would give the Bennets something to talk about. But she also wanted to see him. She wanted to see if he was still thinking about yesterday like she was. She wanted to see if he was also wondering how soon they could get together again.

Just after ten o'clock, she got one of her wishes. Nick entered, and then stopped in the doorway. His eyes sparkled as they ran over her. She drank him in. Crisp chinos and dress shirt, hair artfully tousled. Chiseled cheeks shaved nice and smooth. He really was beautiful. And for one heart-stopping moment, she felt like there were no other two people in the world.

She indicated one of the unoccupied tables close to the windows with a lift of her chin, and then walked toward him. He sat and waited, leaning back to put his arm over the empty chair beside him.

"Can you sit?" he asked.

Oh, how she wanted to. She wanted to cuddle up beside him and lean against the strong arm draped over that vacant chair. Being so close to him again, she could nuzzle his neck and breathe him in. *Careful, Chloe. Don't be a fool.*

"No." She gave a quick shake of her head. "Busy."

His smiled dimmed a little but his gorgeous eyes still twinkled. "What's good today?"

"What do you want?"

"Mmm." He shifted in his seat and leaned forward. "I want what I had yesterday."

A flush spread over her skin and her breath caught. *Oh, my.*

He laughed softly and grabbed a menu from the holder on the table. Giving it a much shorter look than the one he'd given her, he nodded. "The turkey bacon omelet, then."

Once more on safer ground, Chloe relaxed a bit. "Coffee?"

"Sounds good."

"Try the chocolate chip muffins, young man!" Jane Bennet called from her table. "They made our Chloe positively glow this morning."

Nick blinked at them. "Thanks, ma'am. Maybe I will."

Chloe shook her head and blew out a breath. "Don't listen to them."

"Were you glowing this morning?" he asked with a grin.

"Never mind. Do you want a muffin?"

"Is that what we're calling it now?"

She closed her eyes and silently prayed for strength. She went to the service counter and stood for a moment, grateful that the place was otherwise empty for now. Oh, what that man could do to her with just a glance! It was both new and familiar, and it scared her senseless.

She turned the straws in their holder until the seams of their wrappers all faced the same direction, counting them off in her head as she did so. When she finished she felt like she had allowed enough time for her heart to slow to a rate closer to normal. *Sheesh.*

She grabbed the coffee pot and brought it over to him. She could feel his gaze on her as she carefully poured coffee into his cup.

"So other than breakfast, why are you here?"

"I'm meeting a realtor at her office at eleven, to discuss some properties in the area."

She straightened. "A realtor?"

"Yeah. Your brother recommended her, actually."

"Oh." *Krissy.* Jack had told her he'd given Nick her card. She swallowed around the sudden lump in her throat. "Your omelet should be out in a few minutes."

His brows were drawn together over those crystal blue eyes. "What's wrong?"

She shook her head and left his table. Disappointment and a whole lot of other feelings churned in her stomach. She forced herself to set the coffee pot down gently. He was meeting with Krissy. Today.

"Well, that was fun while it lasted."

Krissy would flip her bottle-blonde hair and flash her porcelain veneers and Nick wouldn't bother with Chloe again. So much for having a little passion in her life, if only temporarily. The memory would have to last her until the next time she was foolish enough to fall for someone like him.

"When Hell freezes over," she muttered.

"What did you say?" Jeanine asked.

Chloe shook her head. "Just facing up to reality, Jeanine."

The girl put down the pot of decaf she held. "What about reality?"

Chloe managed a small smile. "It bites."

Chapter 6

Nick wiped his mouth with a napkin and pushed the empty plate away from him. Another great meal at the Cloud Café, although today the service was a little uneven. When he'd stepped into the place, Chloe had looked happy to see him for a hot second. It did a man good to see that heat in a woman's eyes, knowing he was the one guy who put it there. There was the little matter of the three old ladies sitting on the other side of the café, though. Three pairs of eyes ran slowly over him and he didn't know what to make of the arch of their gray brows. They couldn't have meant what he'd thought they did. It was just about the muffins, right? Chloe had blushed, and he couldn't help but feel pretty damn good that he was the reason she was "glowing" today.

When he'd mentioned his meeting with the realtor she'd quickly frozen over, though. Maybe she didn't want him for the couple of weeks she'd offered yesterday. Maybe she just wanted him to get out of Cloud Canyon today. Tough. Ain't gonna happen. They had a deal, even if he had to dance to her tune for the time-being. Or something like that.

He stood and placed a twenty dollar bill on the table. Chloe hadn't given her the check and Nick wasn't going to hold his breath hoping that she would come back to his table this morning. The red-head had delivered his omelet and refilled his coffee after Chloe's freeze-out. He turned and headed for the door.

"Nick, wait."

Then he saw Chloe near the service counter, her eyes wide. There were fewer customers in the place, but the three old ladies still sat there. Nick could hear the faint sound of dishes and utensils rattling and heavy metal music coming from the kitchen where Chloe's staff probably washed dishes and prepped for lunch.

"Yeah?"

She motioned him over and he joined her there.

"I thought we could… Well, later if you like, we can get together."

"Well, yeah." Nick leaned his head toward her and smiled. "You know I want to see you."

Her smile was brief, sparkling bright but gone in an instant. "Let me know if you still want to meet up after your meeting. I'll be here until around four."

He stepped closer and could feel the electricity between them. When her pupils dilated, he knew she felt the same thing. Yeah, he wanted to see her. Why the hell wouldn't he?

"Let you know?" he asked.

"You might get busy." She shrugged and her gaze shifted away from his. "Or something."

"Not too busy to see you."

He let her take that as she wanted. She might not know that she was his prime reason for staying in Cloud Canyon, she and their son. But she had to know that as long as her offer stood he would happily dance to any tune she played.

"Nick, I—"

"Oh, Chloe dear," one of the old ladies called.

Chloe blinked. "Yes, Charlotte?"

"The check, dear. When you get a moment please?"

They smiled and turned to him. Their eyes ran slowly over his body this time. They looked like they wanted to pinch his cheeks and maybe grab his butt.

"I'll be right with you ladies," Chloe said.

"No hurry, Chloe," one said.

"Just happy to sit and chat," another said.

They continued to stare at him and Chloe.

"It seems our Chloe has a new young man," he heard one lady say. "Maybe she won't need those muffins after all."

"Chloe won't give him a tumble," one of them answered.

"Pity," another said. "He's dreamy."

Nick saw that flush of pink rush up Chloe's neck to flood her cheeks.

Grinning, he leaned closer to Chloe. "I'll see you later."

Chloe gave him a smaller smile this time and turned to the old ladies. "I'll go get your check, ladies."

The three woman nodded their silver heads. "Who is that young man, Chloe?"

"Are you dating?"

"Oh, he's very handsome."

Nick could still hear them peppering Chloe with questions as he opened the door and stepped through.

"Good luck with that," he said to himself with a smile.

Nick got into his truck and pulled away from the curb. The realtor's office was a few blocks from the café and he parked in a space out front. Mountain Realty must do a good business, as it filled all of what probably used to be six separate storefronts of the strip it occupied. Newer SUVs and luxury cars were parked off to one side, testament of the success of the company and its realtors. Good. He needed a company used to dealing with more than just private real estate buying and selling. Commercial deals meant lots of money changing hands as well as more complicated contracts.

He walked into the office and stepped up to the receptionist seated at the wide granite-topped desk. "Hi. I have an eleven o'clock appointment with K. L. Bates."

The receptionist, an older woman with dark hair, nodded. "Please have a seat."

Nick thanked her and sat in one of the plush leather chairs that ringed the outer office. Shades of greens and browns decorated the room, and the effect of bringing in the view from outside the wide windows was pleasing.

He leaned back and glanced out the window, but he couldn't see the Cloud Café from his vantage point. It was weird how Chloe had become distant and cool when he'd mentioned his meeting today. Thank God she still wanted to see him this afternoon. She honestly thought he wouldn't want to see her? Yesterday he could have held on to her forever.

He thought about those saucy little old ladies in the café. They were probably just as protective of Chloe as her brother was. That sobered him. She had a lot of people in Cloud Canyon looking after her. Him? He was a stranger, just passing through for all they knew. Hell, didn't Chloe think the same thing?

She had offered him a fling, an affair while he was in Cloud Canyon, and nothing more. She refused to let him apologize for something he couldn't even remember clearly. But what about their son? Nick had to see him. He had to find a way to wear down her defenses where Josh was concerned. Maybe after they got a little bit closer? Although there was nothing closer than what they'd shared yesterday.

"Nick?" a female voice said from the hallway.

Nick turned to find the woman from the business card walking toward him. *Nick?* That was a little forward.

He stood. "Yes."

She stopped and flicked her blond hair over one shoulder of her pink suit jacket, tilting her head. "You don't remember me, do you?"

"I'm sorry, no."

"Krissy Bates." She stepped closer. "From Reno?"

Nick froze. *No. God, no.*

She laughed and waved her hand. "Well, it has been six years."

Krissy. The girl he'd put between himself and Chloe. The drunken mistake he couldn't quite remember.

"You're a realtor," he stated.

She smiled. "One of the best in the office."

He thought for a moment. He had a couple of memories of Krissy, but they were miniscule. He'd met her at the same time he'd met Chloe, but until he'd woken up next to her in bed he hadn't even talked to her all that week. Chloe's strange coolness made sense now. *Nick, you're a fool.*

"Listen, maybe I should work with another realtor."

"I'm a professional, Nick. Come into my office and I'll show you some of the properties I was able to locate after our chat this morning."

Nick saw no sign of the party girl she'd been in Reno. She was all business and that was just what he needed. It wouldn't hurt to see what she'd found out. If she started acting like anything more than a realtor, he would just switch to someone else in the office. He wasn't going to take the chance of ruining what was only just starting with Chloe.

"All right."

"Now you need a large piece of property." She waved him into her office and grabbed up a few papers from her desk. "I've done some preliminary searches and printed out some interesting prospects."

Nick sat in the chair in front of her desk and took the papers she handed him. Topographic maps and carefully-drawn surveys accompanied each listing.

"I'll have to see these. Stockton is new to this area, but I think I'll know what I want when I see it."

"Of course."

Nick faced her again and the only thing he saw in her eyes were dollar signs. That was what he needed from her. Eyes on the prize.

"I visited the National Forest," he said. "I saw a few things I'd like to emulate with the new development."

"What did you have in mind?"

The images that had struck him during his conversation with Chloe's brother came back to him. "A community of cabins, something that would blend in with the land and offer the perfect escape for the owner."

"Hmm." Krissy sat back and chewed on the end of her pen. "Rustic. Refreshing. Breathtaking."

"Yes, all that. For people looking for something other than glitz. But luxurious, too. Rich woods and granite counters. Wired for high-tech and superior sound. Rustic but upscale and very comfortable."

Her eyes lit up as she grasped his idea. "Yes! There's nothing quite like that around here. An exclusive community of, what, thirty or forty cabins? Each with the feel of a private getaway."

"That's about right. But we'd have to find the perfect spot for it. And I'd like to preserve as much of the wilderness as we can around each cabin."

"That should play well with the conservationists." She smiled then. "Stockton Homes will clean up."

Nick nodded. But should he work with her given their past connection? Not to mention his present involvement with Chloe? It was true that he didn't quite know where that involvement would lead, but Krissy sure was a complication they didn't need.

"Listen, Krissy. After whatever happened in Reno, I don't know if we should work together."

"That was a long time ago, Nick. I promise this time will work out much better for both of us."

He flushed. He couldn't even remember doing her, but apparently he'd been less than stellar. "I know I was drunk."

She held up her hand. "We both were. I'm to blame for that mistake, though. And for what happened after."

That morning Chloe had found him in bed with Krissy was suddenly as fresh as if it just happened. He'd been suffering a pounding headache, and nausea and guilt had clawed at him until he could do nothing but watch Chloe storm out of his life. He hadn't even known they'd had a son because of that screw-up.

"Believe me," he began, "over the past six years I've had a lot of time to regret that mistake and what happened after."

"Chloe hasn't spoken to me since, Nick." Her mouth turned down at the corners. "She was my best friend up until then. I sent her a gift when she had her little boy, but she sent it back unopened."

Nick winced at the mention of the son he had yet to see. Apparently Krissy didn't miss his reaction.

She gasped. "Oh, God. He's yours!"

"Yes, he is. And I didn't know about him until yesterday thanks to what happened in Reno that last morning."

Krissy touched his hand briefly, the gesture one of comfort and nothing else. "I'm so sorry." She gave him a small smile. "But now that you'll be in Cloud Canyon for a while, maybe things can be different."

Nick's eyes pricked and he cleared his throat. "Maybe. How soon can you show me these properties?"

"Just let me make a few phone calls."

As she spoke on the phone Nick thought about that long-ago morning. He had to make amends. He had to prove to Chloe that he would never make that mistake again. He'd thrown away happiness with both hands back then, but what if the fates had somehow deemed him worthy of one more chance?

He sure as hell wasn't going to blow it this time.

Chapter 7

"So tell me. Who is he?"

Chloe brushed a stray hair out of Josh's eyes and faced her mother. "Who?"

She stepped out of Josh's earshot and waved her over toward a corner of her antique shop. "The 'hottie' Jeanine told me about," she whispered.

"Mom, please."

"All right." Carol Butler put her hands on her hips. "The guy you couldn't keep your eyes off of on Tuesday."

"Mom, he isn't worth talking about."

"And this morning, if Jeanine could be believed."

Chloe blew out a breath. "Darn Jeanine, anyway. Why can't she be quiet and sullen like a normal twenty-year-old?" She shook her head. "He's nobody that matters. Mom."

Her mother clicked her tongue. "I don't believe that for a second. Don't you think Jeanine told me who he looks like?"

Oh, no. "Thor?" Chloe offered.

"Who? No." Her mother flicked her eyes in Josh's direction. "You know who I mean."

"Look, he doesn't matter."

"Who, Mommy?" Josh asked, his brow furrowed.

Chloe crossed to Josh and dropped a kiss on his forehead. "Nobody, honey. Grandma was just talking about a new customer."

"Oh." Josh turned back to the afternoon cookie snack in front of him. "The Bennies were here. No new cust'mers."

"The Bennet sisters?" Chloe asked her mother. "What tales did they spin?"

Her mother's brow was drawn. "They just confirmed what I feared."

Chloe walked over to a sideboard laden with sparkling crystal. There were blues and reds and greens, and the colors reminded her of Laurel's artwork. She shifted the pieces around until they were arranged by size. Then she took a breath. "You have nothing to be afraid of, Mom."

"No?" Her mother stepped closer and put her hand over Chloe's to still her. "Does he know?"

Chloe's shoulders slumped and she withdrew her hand with a pat. "He does now."

"So now what?"

"Now nothing. It changes nothing."

"How can you say that?"

She faced her mother. "He saw a picture, Mom. In Jack's wallet. He saw a picture and figured it out. He knows now. So what?"

"Then why is he here?"

She thought about his meeting today with Krissy, not wanting to even think about how that had gone. "He's looking for real estate, believe it or not."

"Real estate. Wait. Not with…?"

She nodded. "Yep. They had a meeting today. So rest assured, he won't be coming to the café again."

"Why do you say that?"

She couldn't help but flash back to how she'd found him that morning in Reno, his hair mussed and his face sleepy with Krissy draped all over him. *Because he'll be doing Krissy every chance he gets.* "Because he'll be too busy."

"Chloe."

She hated the pity she heard in her mother's voice. She hated how pitiful she felt to lose something she didn't even want right now. "Please, Mom." She forced a smile. "I'll be fine."

Her mother looked over at Josh who was occupied with his coloring book. "You weren't last time."

"Yeah, well I was young and stupid the last time. Now I'm older and... less stupid."

Her mother's smile was small but heartening. "You're not stupid. And if he isn't, he'll stick around."

"I hope he doesn't."

She clicked her tongue. "Now who's spinning tales? Chloe, you both made mistakes in Reno. But we wouldn't have that wonderful little boy if it wasn't for him."

"I know that." She took in a breath. "I know. But I won't let him have my heart again."

"So just your body?"

"Mom!"

She held up her hands. "You're right. You're a big girl now. But he has rights, you know. Please don't do anything that could bite you on the butt later."

"Trust me, Mom. After today, I'll never hear from him again."

Her mother stared for a long minute, then nodded.

"Josh, honey. What do you say to having dinner with me tonight? We can get a pizza?"

"Pizza? Sure!"

And just like that her mother gave her the evening, free and clear. Chloe doubted she would need it, though. A glance at her watch told her it was nearly four o'clock. Within the hour, her disappointment would be eclipsed by the confirmation that she'd known what was coming all along. It was cold comfort, but still.

Chloe crouched down and gave Josh a hug. "Be a good boy for Grandma, honey. I'll pick you up later."

"If he needs to stay over, that's okay."

Chloe let out a breath. "Mom, please."

"Go on," she said. "We'll be fine."

Chloe stood, letting her gaze run over her little boy. He was her very heart. Josh had no clue what was going on, and now she knew what they meant by "blessed ignorance."

"I'll see you guys tonight," she said.

"Bye, Mommy," Josh said.

Chloe left her mother's shop and walked slowly back toward the café. Her watch showed four o'clock on the dot now and her heart tripped. Would Nick really come back again? After today? She hated feeling like some silly girl, hoping her high school crush would give her some attention now that the head cheerleader had flicked her hair in his direction.

She couldn't see Krissy's office from here, but Nick couldn't still be there anyway. Didn't he say his appointment was at eleven? She didn't want to think about him with Krissy. Not today or on the morning she'd found them in bed together.

God, how stupid she'd been. She'd felt like she'd been on a five mile hike without any water, queasy and dizzy and completely spun around. If he slept with Krissy again, she didn't know what she would do.

"You have no claim on him, Chloe," she told herself as she walked back into the café. "Not then and not now."

"Good, you're back." Jeanine draped her apron on the service counter. "I didn't want to just take off."

"Sorry, Jeanine. I was just talking to my mother."

"No prob. I'll see you tomorrow. Ricky, you wanted a ride home today so come on."

"Yeah, yeah. I'm coming," the dishwasher said from the kitchen. The lanky seventeen-year-old followed his sister out the front door and Chloe locked it behind them. She drew the lacy shade down.

"I'm all set, Chloe," Tom poked his head out of the kitchen.

"Okay, Tom. Thanks."

The big cook nodded and disappeared out the back. The café was dead quiet as she walked into the kitchen. Tom's work station was spotless and Ricky had left only a few suds in the bottom of the big stainless sink. She refrained from wiping the spots away as she passed it to lock the back door. The stairway to the apartment winked into view, forcing her to think about what she'd done after she'd dragged Nick up there. She'd never been so impulsive before, not even back in Reno with the guy.

She turned off the kitchen lights and went back into the dining room. Was she a fool to wait around for Nick? She stepped behind the service counter and began to wipe it down with some lemon oil. The motion soothed her but the scent brought another memory to her mind, to Tuesday afternoon when Nick had pressed her against the counter and started all of this up again with his kisses. She glanced at her watch again. It was almost four thirty and she was finished waiting around like some wallflower.

"Krissy strikes again," she muttered. "At least in Reno I had a whole week."

She stopped at the door and just breathed in. Josh was with her mother and she had nothing demanding her attention for the next few hours. Maybe she would drop in on Laurel at her studio. At least she wouldn't have to pretend around her sister-in-law. Laurel knew full well what Chloe felt for Nick, then and now. Maybe she would confess about yesterday, too. She knew she could count on Laurel to keep Jack in the dark about that little tryst in the apartment.

She left the café and locked the door behind her.

***

Nick nodded to something Krissy said as he walked her back to her car. They had stopped back at her office after grabbing lunch on the road near some farther-flung properties and he'd decided to follow her in the Ridgeline to this location. After spending a few hours with her, he was grateful her perfume wouldn't stink up his truck. It was nothing like Chloe's scent. Chloe smelled like wildflowers and cinnamon. Would he see her tonight? Man, he hoped so.

"And the owners live out-of-state, so there shouldn't be a problem getting them to close quickly," she said.

Nick refocused on Krissy. "Good." He'd spoken to Fred Bennet that morning and learned that he offered business services to inn guests, including printers and scanners if he needed them. "Could you send me the listings?" He glanced at his watch. Shit, it was nearly five. "I'm staying at the Treetop Inn, but you have my email."

Krissy nodded and opened her car door. "Will do. We'll follow up in a couple of days?"

"Sure."

She got into her car but Nick didn't wait for her to drive off. Gravel spun beneath his wheels as he turned back toward Cloud Canyon. He'd told Chloe he would see her this afternoon and now he'd probably missed his chance.

When he pulled up in front of the café it was five thirty. "Nick, you're an idiot," he muttered. He got out of the truck and walked to the front door. He rapped on the glass with his knuckles and waited like yesterday, but he couldn't hear anyone moving around inside. He couldn't see anything but dark beyond the lace shades on the windows. He knocked again but Chloe didn't come to the door. Resting his head on the cool glass window, he blew out a breath.

She'd seemed so unsure this morning. She'd seriously thought he would meet with Krissy for his appointment and then blow her off later? As if Krissy held any appeal after the afternoon he'd shared with Chloe yesterday. But now that he'd missed her at the café? Whatever they had seemed to be over before it even got started. Just like Reno.

God, he'd missed his chance with her. Again. Now he had nothing. Not tonight with her. Not two weeks to see what they could be together. And not a chance to ever get to know his son.

He slammed his fist against the doorjamb. "Damn it!"

"Dude, the café will open again in the morning," a voice drawled to his right.

Nick lifted his head to find a big guy standing on

the sidewalk. He looked familiar and in the next instant Nick recognized him as the other guy who'd stared him down in the café that first day. This guy's hair was lighter than Chloe's and her brother's, but he was undoubtedly a Butler. You couldn't miss those eyes.

Nick straightened. "Hey."

"Hey, yourself." The guy stuck out his hand. "Bo Butler."

Nick saw that Bo wore a navy T-shirt that read "Butler Service and Body" over the left breast pocket.

He shook Bo's hand. "Nick Stockton."

Bo's eyes were sharp. "Were you looking for Chloe?"

"Yes."

"Huh." Bo glanced at Nick's Ridgeline. "Nice ride. Smooth lines. I noticed this truck around town the past couple of days." He looked back at Nick. "You're stayin' at the Treetop?"

On the surface it seemed like an innocuous question, but Nick sensed there was more to Bo Butler than met the eye. "Yes, I am."

Those eyes so like Chloe's narrowed then the big

guy nodded. "Well, Jack asked me to pick up Laurel."

"Laurel?"

"Yeah. Jack's wife. She owns the art studio and gallery down a ways. You know Jack, don't you Nick? Chloe's brother?"

Yeah, Nick knew Jack. And Nick also knew that Bo knew he knew Jack. He simply nodded.

Bo grinned as he shook his head. "Laurel has buckets of money yet she insists on driving that little Beetle even I can't keep running."

"Maybe it has sentimental value."

"Sentimental? Yeah, that's our Laurel. Chloe, too." Bo's expression seemed carved in stone now. "Tough on the outside but mush on the inside."

Nick heard the unspoken warning in Bo's words. Chloe could be soft and vulnerable, but only when she let down that prickly guard of hers. And after Nick's screw-up today? He had no hope of ever seeing that soft and tender side of her again.

"Well, nice meeting you," Nick said.

Bo Butler stood there, his feet braced apart, as Nick climbed into the truck and headed back to the inn. Chloe had family that cared about her. Family that would protect her no matter what. That meant Nick's son had that, too.

He'd have to content himself with that knowledge. Now he had to face the fact that he would never get the chance to care for and protect either Chloe or their son.

Not now.

Chapter 8

"Wow." Bo pulled open the door to Laurel's shop. "That guy has it bad."

Chloe faced her cousin. "Who?"

Bo tilted his head to one side. "That pretty boy."

She felt her heart jump up to her throat and then tumble back down into her stomach. "Who, Bo?"

"Nick Stockton, he said his name was."

"When, um…" Chloe brushed her hair back from her face with a shaky hand. "When did you see Nick?"

"Just now. Outside the café."

"Really? Nick was here?" Laurel leaned past Bo to peer out the window. She looked back at Chloe. "Hmm."

Chloe saw the sparkle in her sister-in-law's hazel eyes. "It doesn't mean anything."

"No?" Laurel turned to Bo. "So, Bo. How would you say Nick looked out there? Happy?" She wiggled her eyebrows. "Satisfied?"

Chloe gasped. "Laurel!"

"Satisfied?" Bo asked. "What do you mean?"

"Laurel, no," she warned.

"Did he look satisfied?" Laurel went on. "You

know. Sexually?"

Bo flushed then grinned. "Nope. Not at all. Why?"

Laurel arched a brow at Chloe.

Chloe waved a hand. "He had an appointment with Krissy today."

"With Krissy?" Bo asked.

"He was going to look at a few properties. Guess he found what he wanted."

Bo barked out a laugh. "You think your pretty boy was with Krissy? Believe me, cuz. That guy wasn't with a woman this afternoon. And he definitely wasn't with Krissy."

"How do you know?" Chloe held up a hand. "Never mind. Don't tell me."

"Ah, Krissy," Bo said. "I've had a few appointments with Krissy. I could hardly walk afterwards."

"Bo," Laurel laughed.

"He wasn't with Krissy, Chloe." Bo grew serious. "That look on his face? He wanted to see you, plain and simple. He was totally bummed that he missed you."

"Really? Do you think so? What did he say?" Chloe snorted. "God, I sound like Jeanine."

Laurel laughed. "Tell her, Bo."

"His chin was on the sidewalk when he saw you weren't in the café."

Chloe closed her eyes and let hope fill her for a sweet moment. Nick wasn't with Krissy? He still wanted to see her?

"Looks like she has it bad too, Laurel," Bo said.

Chloe opened her eyes and found the two of them closely watching her. "Never mind," she said again.

Bo walked over to one of Laurel's largest stained glass panels. She could tell he was getting around to something. Bo never browsed in Laurel's gallery.

"You know, Nick is staying at the Treetop," he said.

"Oh?" He was staying at the Treetop. He would be there now, if he'd headed there after stopping by the café. Her mind began to fill with possibilities. Her mother was watching Josh. She had the next few hours free. Should she go see Nick? "You don't say."

"Hmm," Laurel put in. "The rooms at the Treetop are supposedly very comfortable. Luxurious, even."

"Sturdy furniture, too," Bo said. "Big beds."

"Stop it, you two," Chloe said, her cheeks hot.

Bo's eyes twinkled but he hid his grin. "I'll be outside, Laurel."

"Thanks. I'll be out in a minute." After the door closed behind Bo, she turned to Chloe. "So what are you going to do?"

Chloe straightened her shoulders. "What do you think?"

Laurel smiled for a second, and then stepped closer. "Be careful."

"This is just a fling, Laurel. Nothing else."

"Yeah. That's what I thought when I started seeing your brother."

"Nick and me? We're so not you and Jack."

Chloe turned away from her friend's inquisitive gaze. Their love was undeniable. Her feelings for Nick? It wasn't love, no. Uh huh. Not even the puppy love she'd felt in Reno. And his feelings for her? They were as fleeting as they'd been in Reno, she was pretty sure. But at least today he still wanted to see her. Even after spending the day with Krissy.

"I'm meeting Nick at the inn." She let out a breath. "So much for my reputation. I'm glad Josh is too young to understand gossip."

"What gossip? Who will be watching?" Laurel asked.

"Fred Bennet runs the place, Laurel. Of the Cloud Canyon Bennets?"

"Big deal. Even if Fred didn't say a word, and I don't believe he would, those sisters of his would still find out. Heck, you couldn't keep them from finding out if you met Nick in a cave under cloak of darkness. I swear they have radar."

"Then I might as well give them something to gossip about for the next two weeks."

Laurel was quiet for a moment. "Just the next two weeks?" she asked softly.

Chloe nodded. "That's it."

Laurel's lips thinned but she didn't argue. "If you say so."

She could only imagine what more Laurel wanted to say. It didn't matter. Chloe would take these two weeks for what they were and not dream of anything else beyond that.

"Okay, I'll see you later."

"Take care," Laurel said in parting.

Chloe nodded again.

Just the next two weeks. It would have to be enough. She wouldn't let him hurt her again.

About an hour later, Chloe parked her jeep and stepped out onto the sidewalk. Dropping her keys into her bag she looked up at the Treetop Inn. The inn, a three-story Victorian-era structure, was once the largest house in town. The Bennets had been a wealthy family and, even though they used their maiden names now, town lore had it that all three sisters had married well. Chloe knew that the house, clapboard and uncluttered with hardly any of the gingerbread trim that smothered most Victorian homes, had been left to only son Fred Bennet.

For as long as Chloe could remember, it had been run as an inn. Holiday parties were held there now as when she was a child, and it was still a popular place for gatherings large and small. How many, um, trysts had happened under its peaked roof? And it hosted Ladies' Night in the lounge a couple of times a month. Oh, she wished she had a Cloud Nine to fortify her right now. The Treetop's signature drink would go a long way to calming her silly nerves right about now.

Taking a breath, she stepped up onto the porch. She smoothed a hand over her dress. It was easily one of the prettiest piece of clothing she owned, with shades of violet and blue swirling through the gossamer-thin silk over the satin lining and sparkling here and there with tiny opalescent beads. Laurel said she'd designed it just for her when she'd given it to her for her birthday back in April, but Chloe hadn't had any occasion to wear it. That was, before now.

The fabric gathered beneath her breasts then draped to cling in all the right places and Chloe felt incredibly sexy in it. The bra she wore was a deeper purple than the dress as were the panties beneath it. Strappy sandals were on her feet.

After leaving Laurel's studio she'd gone home and showered, even taking the time to dry her hair. She'd left it loose, for once grateful for the waves she and all the Butlers shared. She'd put on makeup too, even mascara and lipstick. Maybe she'd taken more time than warranted, stalling in case she changed her mind. She hadn't, though. She wouldn't.

Yesterday she'd taken control. Of their affair and of

her own life. But that was in her place, in the café. Now she was coming to him. Was she sending the wrong message? Would he think she wanted a relationship while he was in town? She didn't. Absolutely not.

She was making the decision to go to Nick to take the next step and, with it, the responsibility for their affair. If he truly hadn't jumped on Krissy today maybe he did want only her, at least for these two weeks. She had to believe that. If not, she was just a desperate woman throwing herself at the only guy she'd ever truly wanted.

Grabbing the ornate brass door handle, she pulled opened one of the thick oak double doors. She walked into the lobby and stood in the foyer, her eyes on the Oriental rug beneath her feet. She had no idea which room was Nick's. Crossing to the stand holding ads and brochures, she feigned interest in the colorful flyers as she tried to work up her nerve to go up to the front desk and ask.

"Hello, Chloe," a man said from behind her.

She froze, then turned a smile on Fred Bennet. She'd known he wouldn't miss her from his post behind the desk. Those baby-blues peering through his wire-rimmed glasses were just as sharp as his sisters' eyes.

"Hello, Mr. Bennet."

"Fred." He leaned forward, a smile wreathing his round face. "I've known you since you were a tot. Besides, my sisters talk so often of you I feel like we're good friends."

The Bennet sisters talked about her, did they? She would just bet they did. Chloe gave a quick nod. "You should come by the café and join them sometime."

"Those three?" The old man snorted. "I get enough of those magpies at our weekly dinners."

She laughed. "So I'm not the only one blessed with an inquisitive family?"

"Hardly, my dear. The difference between my sisters and me? I've learned to keep my secrets close." He winked. "Purely a defense mechanism, I'll tell you."

"Well, I envy you."

He glanced past her to the stairs, then back at her. "I can keep other secrets close, too."

His direct gaze assured her that he wouldn't tell his sisters about Chloe's visit. Not this time, and not any time.

A rush of warmth made her throat tighten. "Thank you, Mr. Bennet."

"Fred, dear."

"Fred." She waited a beat, and then spoke again. "Um, what's Nick Stockton's room number?"

"Three-oh-eight."

She smiled at him and turned from him to head for the stairs. Her fingers trailed over the polished oak banister as she climbed to the third floor. The hallway was so quiet that the pounding of her heart was the only thing she could hear. She stopped in front Nick's door and raised her hand to knock. She stilled for a second, then rapped sharply on the door.

"Just a minute," she heard Nick call.

Rustling sounds followed, then muffled footsteps as he came to the door. He pulled it open and she relished the look of surprise on his face. She couldn't miss the chance to drink in the sight of the rest of him, though. He only wore jeans, obviously pulled on in haste as they were zipped but not buttoned. His feet were bare as was his gorgeous chest. *Yum.*

"Hi, Nick."

"Chloe." He glanced back into his room and then ran his fingers through his already-mussed hair. He turned back to her. "I didn't expect you."

Her stomach flipped. Oh, no. Not again. "If this is a bad time—"

"No. I was working, that's all." He stepped back to open the door wider. "Come in."

She glanced into the room and saw it was empty. Messy, but empty. She took a few steps inside. Papers covered the bed and the desk was spread with his laptop, a couple of empty cardboard coffee cups, and more papers spilling out of a soft leather briefcase.

Nick grabbed up the papers on the bed. "Info sheets on some properties," he explained. "The realtor—" He straightened and turned to her. "Uh, yeah. You should know that Krissy Bates is the realtor."

"I do know."

Nick put the papers on his desk and closed the laptop. "Listen, Chloe. This?" He gestured to the papers. "This is just business."

All those papers instead of Krissy on his bed might mean that he was serious about the job. Maybe there wouldn't be a repeat of Reno.

She placed her purse on a table near the door. "My

cousin Bo said you stopped by the café?"

"Yeah. I'm sorry I was late. So damn sorry." He crossed to the door and shut it. "I thought I'd missed seeing you."

"Nothing was set in stone."

That apparently made him grin. "Oh no? I can think of something."

She flushed and he laughed softly.

"Jeez, Chloe. When you blush like that you do something to me. Do you know you turn that same shade of pink when you...?"

She flushed hotter and dropped her gaze to the floor. "Nick," she whispered.

He took her hand and led her over to the bed. The heat in his crystal-blue eyes as they ran over her, the promise of what was to come as he sat on the bed in front of her, made her pulse race. She knew she wouldn't regret this time when he was long gone from Cloud Canyon. Nick was pure passion, her passion, at least for these two weeks.

He ran his fingers over the hem of her dress. "This is pretty."

"My sister-in-law Laurel made it for me."

"The blonde." He rubbed the fabric between his fingers. "It seems so delicate."

"Silk is tougher than it looks."

He looked up at her. "Like you."

"Me, tougher than I look?" She shook her head. "No."

"Yes." He placed his hands on her shoulders then trailed his fingers down her arms. "Take it off?"

She smiled at the hunger she heard in his voice. "I thought you liked it."

"Ah, I don't think even silk is tough enough to stand up to what I want to do to you."

She hid her smile then. Oh, he was a smooth talker. She reached up and eased the thin straps of the dress down first one arm then the other. Nick's eyes were hot on her and she could almost feel his gaze touch her skin as she let the dress dangle from one crooked finger. "Okay?"

He licked his lips and a rush of heat spread over her.

"Oh, yeah." He cleared his throat. "Nice underwear."

She grinned and draped the dress over the chair at the desk and, turning back, kicked off her sandals. He reached for her hand and tugged her close again. This time he eased one knee between her thighs and she placed her arms over his shoulders as her body settled against his. Bringing his hands to her face, he stroked her cheeks. His eyes sparkled into hers and she knew with certainty that she wanted to lose herself for these next couple of hours. She wanted to let him have his way and let herself have hers.

She wrapped her hands around his wrists and leaned closer. "Kiss me, Nick."

With a soft moan, he brought his beautiful mouth to hers and kissed her. His lips were soft, his tongue insistent, as he worked his magic on her. His mouth slid over hers as razor stubble gently scraped her skin. He could kiss! She hadn't been so thoroughly kissed since Reno. Not that first day in the café. Not yesterday when she'd dragged him up to the apartment. Oh, his kisses!

He slowly sank his fingers into her hair as he tilted her head to one side. She held on to his shoulders as his mouth left hers to trail down her throat.

"Nick," she breathed.

He pressed his tongue against the hollow of her throat. "I can feel your pulse, Chloe." He kissed the side of her neck. "It's racing."

Nick removed her bra and caressed her. He pulled back and stared at her. "God, you're beautiful. More beautiful than I remember."

"I'm not twenty anymore," she whispered.

"No." He grinned up at her. "Now you're stacked."

She started to laugh until he brought his mouth to her breast. Letting out a sigh, she ran her fingers through his hair and held him there. His lips were magic as he began to suckle. Pleasure stabbed through her, making her want more. It was torture. It was heaven.

"Please, Nick."

He was breathing fast when he pulled away, his cheeks flushed and his hair a wreck from her hands. After another long kiss he leaned away from her. She fell toward him and he turned to tumble her down onto the bed.

"What do you want?" His voice was raspy.

"I want you," she whispered.

He came up and stretched over her body. He was so close, almost inside of her where she wanted him to be. Where she needed him to be.

"And I want you," he said, kissing her neck.

She squirmed beneath him and he growled in response.

"Now." He grabbed a condom from the nightstand and then he was inside her. Deep inside her. She arched toward him as she felt herself shatter.

He kept up the pressure, on and on, until the bed creaked beneath them. He drove her skillfully to her second orgasm. With it, he climaxed too. "God, Chloe!"

She held on to him as he eased down on top of her. She couldn't think as she cuddled against him. When he held her close, dropping kisses on her face, her neck, she didn't pull away. It felt so good.

"Oh, baby." He kissed her again. "That was so worth the wait."

She smiled and snuggled against him for a minute. She would make herself leave his bed soon. She would separate their affair from the rest of her life. Just a few minutes more, though. She couldn't think about leaving his arms right now.

He kissed her cheek and made a sound of intense satisfaction. He sounded way too content. She sat up and crossed her arms in front of her.

"Don't tell me you have to leave." He leaned up on one elbow. "Not yet."

No doubt he was thinking of her swift escape from the little apartment. But tonight was different. "No." She slipped off the bed and grabbed her dress from the chair. "I just want to get dressed." She found her bra on the floor but her panties had to be lost in the folds of the plaid coverlet.

"Chloe." She straightened and found Nick holding them out to her.

She stepped closer and took the panties from him. "Thanks."

He didn't say anything more as she stepped into the bathroom and shut the door. That was close. A few more minutes in Nick's arms and she would forget everything that had happened before. She couldn't let down her guard and let him hurt her all over again. This was what it was and it would have to be enough. She let out a breath.

If only her heart would listen to her head.

Chapter 9

Nick stared at the bathroom door, trying to get his mind to function again. It wasn't easy. He'd put off his own orgasm for the longest time in his memory, but Chloe's sweet moans had made it all worth it. She'd softened there for a minute afterward, cuddled in his arms as they both slowly came back to their senses. But only for a minute, damn it.

He got out of bed and pulled on his jeans. After straightening the quilt, he crossed to the mini bar. He grabbed a couple of mineral waters and cracked one open. As he drank, Chloe came out of the bathroom. She'd obviously tried to control that incredible hair, which now fell in somewhat-tame waves over one shoulder. He could still feel the stroke of that hair through his fingers as he'd kissed her senseless.

He held the other bottle out to her. "Want one?"

She took the bottle and stared up at him with a soft look in her eyes he'd never seen before. Her mouth curved sweetly, and she reached up to run her fingers through his hair. It was such a unconsciously personal gesture that it caused him to still.

She blushed and dropped her hand. "Sorry." She sat on the edge of the bed and opened her water. "Thanks."

What was that about? There was a thread of connection there, something that had been missing as they'd had sex. He turned back to the mini bar. "This isn't like any place I've stayed before. There's some kind of homemade bread here. Some muffins. Chocolate covered popcorn, I think. Not a jar of macadamia nuts or bag of cheese puffs in the place."

"Fred Bennet likes to buy from local vendors. The bakery, the candy shop."

Nick turned the desk chair toward her and sat. "Makes sense. Want something? Or maybe we could grab dinner?"

Her eyes widened for a second and he wouldn't have been surprised if she bolted for the door.

"I…" She swallowed. "I could go for that nut bread."

Nick handed her a wrapped slice of the stuff and popped a mini muffin in his mouth. As he chewed, he watched her pick out the dried fruit to nibble on. He finally broke the silence. "So how long can you stay?"

She paused for a moment then looked him square in the eyes. "I'm free for a couple of hours."

"Really?" He felt a grin curve his lips. "Hours?"

That blush was back on her cheeks. "Yes."

Did that blush cover her whole body? Hmm. He would sure like to find out.

He tilted his head toward the bathroom. "I suppose you noticed that big bathtub in there?"

Her eyes sparkled and she tried to hide her smile behind her bottle.

Nick shifted in his chair. *Hours.* "So where's, um?"

"Josh?" Her voice cooled a little. "My Mom is watching him."

There was no sparkle or blush now. Just prickly Chloe, front and center.

"We can talk about him, you know."

She traced the stitching on the bedspread with one finger. "I know."

Damn right. Nick took another sip of water. "He's five?"

"Yes. His birthday is March 15."

"The Ides of March."

Chloe laughed softly. "He's a force of nature for sure."

He thought of the kid with the mischievous grin peering out of Jack Butler's wallet. "He's beautiful."

"He looks like you."

His heart twisted at the softly-spoken words. "I only saw the one picture."

She got up and reached for her purse, pulling out her phone. Flicking her fingers over the screen, she pulled up a few pictures and handed it to him.

Nick pored over the photos, seeing the sweet little boy he'd had no idea existed just a few days ago. Tears stung his eyes. "Man," was all he could say at the moment.

Chloe played with the ring around the neck of her bottle. "It's strange loving someone who looks exactly like..." She shrugged.

He faced her fully now. "Someone you hate?"

She shook her head. "Someone you don't love." She lifted her head to face him. "I don't hate you, Nick."

"Well, that's something." After another long look at her phone, he handed it back to her. "Is he in school?"

She nodded as she slid the phone back into her

purse. "He goes to Pre-K three days a week but he'll start Kindergarten in the fall. My mom watches him most days. Jack takes him fishing now and then."

"He's lucky to have so much family."

Chloe arched a brow in question. "You don't?"

"I don't have any brothers or sisters. Just my mom, dad and Stockton Homes." He tossed his empty bottle in the trash can. "So no dinner tonight, huh?"

"I don't think so."

Nick leaned back and wiggled his eyebrows. "I'll just be your dirty little secret?"

She smiled. "Maybe. But you really can't keep any secrets in Cloud Canyon."

"Yeah. Good old Fred Bennet looks like he doesn't miss a thing. But come on, Chloe. I can't live on just sex and muffins for the next two weeks."

"Sex and muffins. Sounds like an X-rated bakery."

He chuckled. "We have those in Reno. They can make a cake that looks exactly like your—"

"Never mind." Then she laughed too, a soft throaty sound.

He let his eyes roam over her body. That pretty

dress looked very short with her perched on his bed. He knew her thighs were soft and smooth, especially close to her center.

"I'd rather taste you, though," he said. "Sweet."

He felt another punch of lust and when her pupils dilated he knew she felt it too, that swift return of passion. She fingered the hem of that dress, unconsciously showing him even more of those gorgeous legs.

"Maybe some time we can do dinner somewhere away from Cloud Canyon," she offered.

He thought for a moment. "How about Truckee? That seems about far away enough."

That sparkle was back in her eyes. "Maybe."

Nick stood. "I'm going to order a pizza. Why don't you fill that big bathtub?"

She nodded and went into the bathroom. Nick found a phone book of all things in the top desk drawer and began to flip through it. Tonight, sex and pizza. Maybe one night soon they would have an actual date. Why did it seem like this relationship was working in reverse?

And why wasn't he scared, even a little bit?

The next morning Nick woke up alone in the bed.

Again. But the Egyptian cotton sheets still held traces of Chloe. He buried his face in the pillow and breathed in. Mmm. Even though they'd used almost all the bath gel in the tiny bottle there was still no mistaking Chloe underneath that crisp citrus scent.

He glanced at the clock on the nightstand and saw it was nearly nine. Krissy expected his call this morning regarding the properties she'd sent. Damn it. Krissy.

Once again, he considered using another realtor. He'd seen the doubt on Chloe's face yesterday, seen worry cloud her eyes as she'd obviously wondered if Krissy was in his room. What made her put that all aside, he would never know. But he was grateful she had. She'd stepped into his room and left any doubts outside. Man, when she gave herself she didn't do it half way.

Seeing his son on her phone was surreal, but he'd felt an immediate connection to the little guy. He was a Butler, sure. But there was a lot of him in his son.

He forced himself to get out of the bed and walked into the bathroom. He showered, shaved and dressed before calling Krissy's office.

"K. L. Bates," she answered, her voice crisp.

"Nick Stockton," he said. "I had a chance to—"

"Nick! I'm so glad you called."

He paused, trying to gauge her tone. Was she back to playing party girl or did she have her eyes on the real prize? "I said I would call this morning. I wanted to arrange to see a few properties."

"That's why I'm glad. I spoke with the out-of-state property owners, thank God they're three hours early on the East Coast, and they're amenable to negotiations."

He didn't need to see her to know those dollar signs were back. All business. Good. "I'll need to see the property again."

"Do you need me to come along?"

"No, thanks. I might need directions to some of the other properties, though."

"Sure. Give me the listing numbers and I'll shoot the directions over ASAP."

He ended the call soon after. He glanced down at his clothes. Jeans would be better for tromping through the woods. And maybe a pair of boots. Jeans, boots. He grinned. Maybe some flannel. He should probably stop at the sporting goods store he'd seen in town.

"What would Joe Stockton think of his baby boy now?"

He swapped his chinos for jeans and gathered his papers. He'd shoved them into piles so quickly when Chloe came over he hadn't taken the time to put them in order. After setting the tiny coffee maker on top of the minibar to brew a cup, he sat down at the desk and pored over the property descriptions once more.

The property they'd looked at last, the one with the out-of-state owners, had a lot of potential. He would have to investigate any conservation concerns or protected areas that might encroach close to it, however. Maybe Jack Butler might help put him in touch with the proper agencies. That is, if he didn't find out that Nick was doing his sister. He didn't want to think about what the Forest Ranger would do if he thought Nick was taking advantage of Chloe. He sure as hell wouldn't help Nick do anything to stick around Cloud Canyon. That was for sure.

Nick drank his coffee and sent an email to his father regarding his progress on the land search. Stacking the papers once more, he slid them into his briefcase and stood. He would head over to the Cloud Café for breakfast and a decent cup of coffee, and then maybe hit up the sporting goods store.

But only after he'd had another chance to spend a few minutes with Chloe.

***

As Nick left the café, he let the memory of the little bit of warmth he and Chloe had shared settle in his belly along with the fantastic western omelet he'd eaten. The sporting goods store was located not far from Bo Butler's service station, but he somehow avoided running into any other Butlers on his way. He parked the truck and got out. The store seemed to have just about everything you might need to outfit yourself for spending some time in and around the mountains. He spied kayaks lined up against the back wall and tall and short fishing pole standing in rows along one side.

He stopped in front a rack of flannel in every imaginable color.

"Can I help you?" a woman asked from behind.

He turned and saw she was about Chloe's age maybe, a little bit shorter, and wearing a nametag that read "Josie." She was wearing flannel and jeans and her long dark hair was in a high ponytail. Her eyebrows were arched in question.

"Yeah, thanks. I need a couple of shirts." He snapped his fingers. "And boots. I need good hiking boots I won't have to break in."

She nibbled her lip for a second and then started toward the left side of the store. Nick followed her as she looked over the row of boots. She turned to glance down at his feet.

"I'm assuming you need light hikers?"

"I guess so. I'm not planning any long hikes."

"Size twelve?"

He blinked. "Yeah."

She nodded and handed him a big shoebox. "These should work. Leather uppers, weatherproof but breathable."

"Okay."

"Here." She reached for a pair of thick gray socks. "You'll need these."

He grinned. "Nice upsell."

"Hey," she said with a wink. "I'm good."

"You're also right, I think." He held up the socks and sat on a low bench to try on the boots.

"You're staying at the Treetop, right?" she asked.

"I am, yeah."

"Hmm."

He looked up at her. "You want to ask me something?"

She smiled. "Just that my friend Chloe was at the Treetop last night."

He managed to keep an even expression. "You don't say."

She blinked, and then laughed. "Nice try." Holding up her hands, she shook her head. "Hey, I've only been in Cloud Canyon for about a year. I would never spread rumors that might hurt one of the few friends I have in this town."

"And I wouldn't want to hurt that particular friend, either."

She gave a sharp nod. "Good. So how do those boots feel?"

He stood, stomping a little to get a feel for the new boots. "Nice, Josie. Thanks."

She grabbed his sneakers and threw them into the box. "You're wearing them out, I'm guessing?"

"Yeah, thanks."

She nodded again and, after grabbing a couple of flannels and three Henley shirts, he joined her at the check out counter.

A couple of hours or so later, his newly-booted feet were planted firmly as he held himself still and quiet, letting the sense of the land wash over him. The sun was warm but in the shade of the tall pines around him there was a refreshing coolness. He was glad he'd thrown on one of his new flannel shirts. The smells, earth and pine and a kind of indefinable freshness, filled his lungs. He took another deep breath.

"Amazing. I guess I'm a mountain man now."

After leaving the sporting goods store, and Chloe's friend Josie's probing gaze and questions, he'd spent the day looking at the other properties Krissy had suggested. None suited his vision like this one, though. With the possibility that the owners were open to negotiations, this land was head and shoulders above the others on Nick's short list. It was gorgeous in the morning and this afternoon it almost sparkled.

He laughed to himself. "Jeez, next I'll be writing a

country song."

Turning away from the property, he climbed the slight incline in his new boots to where he'd parked the Ridgeline. Taking out his cell phone he punched in his father's number. As he waited for the connection he climbed into the truck and mentally reviewed what he knew of the property.

It was a little over two-hundred acres, and to his untrained eye it looked like the perfect setting for Stockton's new venture. Forty, maybe fifty, luxury cabins, each surrounded by a buffer due to the one-acre lots and the trees that would be left standing.

"Joe Stockton," his father answered.

"Hi, Dad."

"What have you got?"

Right to business. Nick couldn't help but grin. "I think I've found a property we can use. For the new project."

"Nick, what is this new project? You haven't sent me any specifics yet."

The irritation was there, that and the drive that had made Stockton what it was. Nick felt that same drive wake inside him. If he had to play by his father's rules, so be it. He wanted this project almost as much as he wanted Chloe and their son.

"Cabins, Dad."

He let that settle for a moment.

"Cabins?" His father snorted. "Like those shacks on South Lake Tahoe?"

"Those are hardly shacks, but no. Nothing like those vacation cabins. Think luxury. Convenience. State-of-the-art electronics and mechanics. But rustic, too."

"Rustic? Hmm. Like, log cabins?"

Nick thought for a moment, tracing his finger over the leather laces on the steering wheel. Custom log cabins, exposed beams, wide windows. "Maybe. But they would have to be very distinctive. Nothing cookie cutter."

His father was quiet and Nick held his breath. Yeah, maybe he would have a chance to prove himself to Joe. But if he did, he would also have the chance to stay in Cloud Canyon and see Chloe. And maybe get to know his son.

"You have some talent there, son," Joe finally said. "Why don't you draw up some ideas for our design department and send them over?"

Nick's mouth dropped open but he soon recovered. "Yeah. I'll do that."

"And keep me posted on the property search. You know the drill. Easements, restrictions. Taxes."

"Sure, Dad. I'll get back to you on that, too."

"Fine." Joe was quiet again. "Good work. Talk to you soon."

Nick mumbled his thanks and disconnected the call, his mind working. This would be very different compared to the upscale developments Stockton had completed in the past decade. He saw no need for a recreation center or clubhouse with this one. If what little he'd seen of the National Forest the other day was any indication, there was plenty of recreation to be had if the homeowners were so inclined. One stop at the store in town and they would have everything they would need to find their own entertainment. And the cabins would be so well-designed for every anticipated comfort he doubted they would ever want to leave.

He could envision the ad copy. Healthy, happy people of varying ages rafting or kayaking or hiking. Coming home to their Stockton luxury cabin to curl up in front of a roughhewn fireplace with a state-of-the-art TV hanging above it. Gourmet kitchen and luxurious spa-like bathrooms. Spacious yet cozy bedrooms with angled rooflines and deep eaves.

Hell, if he had one of the cabins he'd have a hard time leaving it. Especially if he had someone to share it with. What would Chloe think of all of this?

The design classes he'd taken in college, along with the business classes Joe had insisted upon, gave him some ability to draw the essentials out on paper. He had to be able to capture the feel of the homes he wanted Stockton to create. Luxury and convenience coupled with the rustic and natural. Then Stockton's design department could draw up several distinctive designs for prospective owners to choose once Nick gave them his ideas.

"Joe's on board?" He punched the cushioned dash and let out a whoop. "Damn, I'm good!"

He started the truck and headed back to Krissy's office. He needed the market analysis on similar properties over the past year and to make sure there weren't any restrictions to build what he envisioned. He didn't want anything to prevent his going forward with his plans in

Cloud Canyon.

Nick thought again about Chloe and their son. No. He wouldn't let anything throw a wrench in his plans.

Chapter 10

Chloe gave the service counter a final wipe. The day's business was over, the place was empty, and for the first time she almost regretted the brisk business the café did. Nick had come in for breakfast and she'd so wanted to join him at his table. They didn't have that kind of relationship, though. Heck, they didn't have any kind of relationship. But that hadn't stopped her stupid heart from skipping when he'd walked into the café that morning. He'd been wearing jeans again, well-worn like the ones he'd had on yesterday, faded in all the best places. He'd looked amazing.

No Nick at lunch time, though. No doubt he was off with Krissy, looking at properties or whatever. Maybe they would get together tonight, maybe not. She wouldn't think about him with Krissy. She wouldn't worry over her own attraction to him, either. Not now. She'd seen how he'd pored over the photos of Josh on her phone and had to admit that he seemed genuinely engaged. Her heart had twisted just a little bit. This morning? One look into those crystal-blue eyes and she'd been sure that he remembered everything they'd done in his room at the Treetop. Oh, and in that bathtub?

The bell above the door jingled and she turned to find Jack standing there. She flushed to think of what had just been on her mind.

She folded the wiping cloth and blew out a breath. "What are you doing here?"

"I was just down at Mom's. She said to tell you she'll take Josh home with her and give him dinner. She'll drop him by your place later."

"Oh." Her mother obviously thought Chloe would take the hint and see Nick again. "Thanks."

Jack stepped closer. "I want to talk to you."

"Uh-oh." She placed the cloth in the laundry bin and walked back to the counter. "Big brother voice."

"Yeah." He glanced toward the back of the café, toward the kitchen. "Are we alone?"

"Yes." She braced her hands on the counter. "What do you want, Jack?"

"I saw you with him, Chloe. This morning."

"Who?"

"Who? Come on. The pretty boy."

"Nick."

Jack waved his hand. "I saw the way he was looking at you. And the way you were looking at him."

She put a hand on her hip. "Is that so?"

"I might be dense about some things."

Chloe snorted. "Yeah."

"Laurel can back you up on that. But I can tell you're thinking about, you know." He trailed off, his eyes suddenly going wide as he saw something change in her expression. "Oh, God. You slept with him, didn't you?"

To her embarrassment her cheeks flushed hot again. She studied the grain of the countertop, running the tip of her forefinger over the dark lines until she'd traced a crooked figure eight. Five times. "I'm not going to talk about this with you."

"What are you thinking?"

She looked up at him in amazement. "You're one to talk. You had sex with Laurel two days after you two met."

"That was different. There was nothing between us."

Chloe raised a brow.

Her brother's lip curled in a half-smile. "There was nothing between us at first," he clarified. "But Laurel and I

couldn't keep our hearts out of it, Chloe. Not for long. Now
I can't speak for the pretty boy—"

"Nick."

His lips thinned. "Nick," he repeated with obvious
reluctance. "But I know you, sis. You'll fall for him again."

His concern for her was clear and her irritation
eased. She stepped closer to Jack, this burly brother of hers,
and smiled up at him. "I know you look all big and tough,
Jack Butler. But you're just a softy inside."

He barked out a short laugh. "And you're saying
you're not?"

She shook her head. "No. Look, I admit it's hard to
separate my affair—"

"Oh, God," he groaned, closing his eyes.

"My affair," she continued as if he hadn't
interrupted her, "with the fact that he's also Josh's father.
But I will."

"How? You're telling me you won't buy his line of
crap again?"

She put a hand on his arm. "Let me deal with my
heart." She gave his arm a pat. "And you might be
interested to know that Laurel told me to 'go for it.'"

Jack's brows raised. "Huh."

"What does that mean?"

Jack shook his head. "Nothing. What about Josh?"

"What about him?"

"He's his son."

"So?"

"So? If I just found out I had a son, you can be damn sure I would want to see him. Now I don't know the pretty boy." Jack held up a hand before she could correct him again, "I don't know Nick, but I'd guess he would want that too."

"We talked about it. He won't see Josh."

"Son-of-a-bitch! How can a guy not want to see his own son?"

"He wants to." Chloe couldn't bring herself to face Jack when she said next. "I won't let him."

Jack was quiet. So quiet Chloe forced herself to look at him. The censure she read in his eyes was worse than his worry. Was she wrong to keep Nick from their son? Again, she thought about Nick's expression as he looked at those pictures on her phone.

"Jack, I…"

Jack shook his head and turned away. "I've said enough. Josh is your son. You know what's best for him." When he got to the door he turned. "Sis, I just…"

Chloe braced herself for his parting words.

"I just want you to be careful," he finished.

Her eyes pricked hot. "I will."

Jack nodded again and left the café. Chloe stared at the door, mulling over Jack's words. He would want to see his son, he'd said. Well, hadn't Nick said that too?

She pulled out a chair at the nearest table and sank down into it. He asked to see Josh the day he found out about him. Should she let him? "No, no, no." She stood with a jerk, causing her chair to clatter to the floor. "I can't. I won't."

Taking a calming breath, she bent and righted the chair. She shifted it until it was the same distance from the table's edge as the others. She blew out the breath.

She couldn't risk Josh coming to count on Nick. She couldn't bear the thought of Josh looking up to someone who would leave Cloud Canyon without looking back.

But what about her?

"My heart. My risk."

She crossed to the door and locked it tight. She turned off the lights and then headed out the back to her Wrangler. Sliding behind the wheel, she thought about yesterday with Nick. Not just the sex part, which had been incredible. But the talking part. He'd danced around the subject of their son but she'd seen the hunger in his eyes as she'd given him the barest details of Josh's life in Cloud Canyon. Nick had seemed eager for any information.

"What am I going to do?" she muttered, letting her head rest on the steering wheel. She breathed in again, long and deep, calming her nerves at last.

Nick wanted to go out to dinner. Tonight. She couldn't. Space was what she needed. Distance from his eyes, his body, his touch. Sharing a meal with him, alone with him, over in Truckee wouldn't help her maintain what little distance she somehow managed to keep around him outside of his room at the Treetop. So no dinner. At least not tonight.

It was Friday, classic date night if she remembered correctly . She just wasn't ready for that. Going to Nick's room at the Treetop was coming dangerously close to implying that she wanted a relationship of some kind with him. A date on Friday night? That would be too much. She had no room in her life for the mess and disruption of an emotional entanglement. Better to keep things as they were now. Neat. Compartmentalized. A place for everything and everything in its place.

It was what had kept her grounded after finding out she was pregnant. It was what had help her stay focused once she discovered her dream to open the café. It would keep her heart out of her affair with Nick now. And she had Josh to consider. What if he grew close to his father and Nick left Cloud Canyon in a couple of weeks like she knew he would? She would do anything to spare her son a fraction of the hurt that would cause.

She started the Jeep, her mind focused on the coming evening. She decided that she would spend tonight with her favorite guy, her Josh. Her mother probably thought she would leave him with her again tonight. Who would have ever thought that her mother would play matchmaker? But Chloe wouldn't let her. No. She would swing by her mother's and then head home.

As she drove past the Treetop Inn she slowed. With

a jerk of the wheel she pulled next to the curb and braked. She switched off the motor and sat for a long minute. She should tell Nick she wouldn't be able to join him for dinner. They hadn't shared cell numbers, not that service was reliable here in the mountains. She smiled. It was only polite, after all. Her mother hadn't raised her to be rude, right?

She got out of the Jeep and went into the inn.

***

Nick leaned back in the chair and glanced at his watch. Almost five-thirty.

"Do you have to go?" Krissy asked.

"I'm supposed to go to dinner." He shook his head. "Well, we didn't settle on a time, actually."

Krissy nodded and pulled a few sheets of papers off the printer tray. "Here are the last of the market comparisons."

"Great." He took the papers and slid them into his briefcase. "I'll go over these and the documents from the county tonight."

"When do you think you'll want to make a move?"

"I have to send the info over to Stockton's legal

department to double-check everything." He smiled. "Triple-check, really. But as soon as I have the go ahead to make the offer, I'll be in touch."

"Terrific."

Nick started to stand then stilled. "Oh. I had a question about recreation."

"Recreation? You mean, amenities in the development?"

"No. My preliminary plans don't include a rec center in the development. I wondered where I could get info on all the recreation available in the surrounding area."

"Well, the Tahoe National Forest has a terrific website. Tons of info on activities. Fees and stuff."

"Cool. I'll get the address off the brochure."

"Why don't you talk to Jack Butler?"

"Chloe's brother, the Forest Ranger? Why?"

"He's not just a Ranger. Jack is the Director of Recreational Management for the district."

"Really?" Nick blew out a breath. "Yeah, he would probably be a great resource, but talking with him could be difficult."

"Jack knows more about the Forest than anyone in

the district."

Nick sensed something about the way she said the guy's name. "Were you and Jack ever a thing?"

To his amazement Krissy blushed. "Yes, sort of. After his divorce. And not for very long."

"But, the blonde I saw him with. Isn't she his wife?"

Krissy laughed softly. "Now. This was years ago. Laurel is just lovely. His first wife, though?" She clicked her tongue. "And people call me a bitch. I helped him when he was buying his ex-wife out of their cabin after their settlement."

"Jack has a cabin?"

"Yes." Her eyes widened. "Oh! You should see Jack's cabin. It's rustic, much smaller than what you're thinking of for Stockton, but it has several of the elements you mentioned. Granite counters, custom cabinetry, wide windows. And the views. Wow."

"Huh." Nick thought about the last time he'd seen Jack, in the café just that morning. Those blue-gray eyes had drilled into Nick's skull every time Chloe stopped by his table. "I doubt Jack will invite me over for a couple of beers and to catch a game any time soon."

Krissy shrugged. "Maybe Chloe can ask him to help you out." She held up a hand. "Never mind, Nick. Sorry. None of my business."

Nick shook his head and stood. "No problem. I'll be in touch."

He left her office and headed back to the inn. Chloe was probably long gone from the café by now and he had no idea how to get in touch with her. She wanted to keep things light and easy, and that meant not sharing cell numbers. Fred Bennet would know where she lived, though. The guy knew pretty much everything.

"Yeah, that would work." There was no way Nick would just show up on her doorstep. That was just the thing to spook her from ever letting him see their son, let alone continue whatever it was they had going on now.

Nick parked in front of the inn. He grabbed his briefcase out of the truck and climbed the steps.

Fred Bennet looked up as Nick entered the lobby, a smile on his face. "Mr. Stockton!"

Nick walked over to the front desk. "Nick, Mr. Bennet."

"Ha! Nick, then." Fred nudged his glasses up on the bridge of his nose. "Fred, please. I have a note for you."

Nick eyed the folded piece of paper, apparently one of the sheets of ivory stationery emblazoned with the Treetop's logo. "Who's it from?"

Fred winked. "Now I'm not one to carry tales, Nick."

Nick's pulse jumped and he grabbed the note from him. "Thanks, Fred."

Turning from the desk he unfolded the note. It was from Chloe. He read that she wouldn't be able to have dinner with him tonight but before disappointment could strike too hard he saw that she'd written her cell number at the bottom. Grinning like a fool, he slipped the note into his breast pocket.

Taking the steps two at a time, he went up to his room. He called Chloe's number but she didn't answer so he left her a voicemail message. He went through the papers in his briefcase and then paced the length of the room, glancing at the clock on the nightstand. Twenty minutes already. What was taking Chloe so long to call him back?

He stilled, laughing. "What am I, sixteen?"

He couldn't just sit around and wait for her call. After taking a shower, he sat in front of his laptop and drafted the proposal to send to his father at Stockton. Referring to the information from Krissy and the county, and his own notes on the property, he put together a succinct report. He knew Joe wouldn't want any flowery words or fancy descriptions, just the hard facts of the company's possible liabilities and potential gains. Then, when the time came, they would leave it to the sales staff at Stockton to come up with the press releases, glossy ads, and killer website devoted to the project.

He emailed the proposal to his father and closed the laptop. Setting it aside, he thought again about his ideas for the project.

"I'd love to get a look at Jack Butler's cabin." He snorted. He hadn't been kidding when he'd told Krissy that wouldn't happen any time soon. "The guy would probably shoot me on site."

Grabbing up some of the information sheets on the properties he'd seen and dismissed, he flipped them over and cleared off a spot on the desk. "Pen, pencil…" He pulled open the shallow desk drawer and found a couple of pens inside. "That'll work."

Smiling to himself, he began to sketch out his ideas.

Chapter 11

Nick shifted the papers around on the desk, frustrated that he couldn't get the look he was after. He needed some direction to focus his inspiration, and sitting in the cozy room wasn't doing it for him. It didn't help matters that Chloe lingered in every corner. She still hadn't called him back and it was after eight. He didn't dare call her again, since she was probably tied up with their son.

Their son. What stories did Josh like to hear before bed? Nick had fond memories of his own bedtime rituals. Joe seemed to always be working but Nick's mom had made sure he never felt alone. Chloe probably took terrific care of Josh. She didn't do anything half-way. Josh was a lucky little kid to have her as a mom.

He reached for the phone again, and then clenched his hand. "I gotta get out of here."

He grabbed his leather jacket and left the room, bound for the lobby. He found Fred there as usual, but instead of his customary post behind the desk he was sitting in front of the wide gilded fireplace with a book in his hands. The old guy must live in the place, too.

"Hey there, Nick."

"Hi, Fred." Nick put on his jacket. "Is there any place that stays open past seven around here?"

"Bored, are you?" Fred closed his book. "No visitors tonight?"

Nick flushed. "Not tonight."

"Hmm. She's a busy gal, you know."

Nick didn't need the man's kind words but it felt good to know that Chloe was a devoted mother. Even if that devotion kept her from him tonight.

"I just wanted to grab something to eat. Maybe have a drink."

"The Antler, then. The bar over on US 80."

"So outside of Cloud Canyon?"

"Yep. Just past the turnoff for Soda Springs."

"What kind of place is it?"

"Like you'd think. Liquor, some food. Music. Pool table."

"Local hangout?"

"Mostly. And vacationers not too tired out from the Forest."

He thought for a minute. It could be good to soak up some of the local vibe, even if the bar crowd wasn't his target demographic for the luxury cabins he envisioned. He thanked Fred and headed out to his truck.

Following along US 80, Nick found The Antler as Fred promised. The building resembled an oversized shack, and its gabled roof was strung with holiday lights and bright neon signs hung in just about every window. The parking lot was nearly full, which was no surprise on a Friday night. He stepped around a couple making their leisurely way to their car and pulled open the heavy door at the entrance of the bar.

There was more neon in here, and the thrum of the jukebox underscored the sounds of laughter and conversation. The space was squat and wide, with dimly-lit booths along the windows on the front wall and a bar taking up most of the space on the back. Over to the right was a pool table and a few old arcade games.

His first impression of the crowd was of flannel and denim and one or two cowboy hats. Nick was pleased to see no one smoking, and the heavy smells of beer and fried foods weren't unpleasant. The Antler was a far cry from the Cloud Café, but he was having enough trouble keeping Chloe from his mind anyway.

He made his way through the crowd to the bar. The guy behind it nodded and looked at him in question.

"Bud in a bottle, please."

The bartender opened the bottle and set it front of Nick. "Start a tab?"

Nick took a pull on the beer. "Sure." He sat on the leather stool and set his arms on the bar. A guy three stools down caught his eye and he turned toward him. Butler-blue eyes stared back at him. *Bo Butler*. Nick saluted him with his bottle and took another sip.

Out of the corner of his eye he saw Bo stand and make his way over. Nick faced him. "Bo."

"Nick." Bo set down his beer mug and propped an elbow on the bar. "What's up?"

He knew that the guy was really asking about Chloe, and wanted to know what was up with the two of them. Nick wasn't going to touch that subject with her cousin, though. Nope.

"Nothing much," he answered.

Bo sat on the stool beside him. "Nothing on for tonight?"

"Not a thing."

Bo studied him and once again Nick had the impression that there was more to this Butler than he let on. A pair of feminine arms circled Bo's neck and Bo stiffened. "Krissy."

Krissy nuzzled Bo's ear, then she spotted Nick and put on that professional face he'd come to expect. "Nick!"

"Hi, Krissy."

Bo feigned interest in his beer mug but Nick could tell he was watching their exchange. What had Chloe told her family about Nick and Krissy? About that morning in Reno?

"What are you doing here?" she asked.

"Just grabbing a beer."

"Have you put together Stockton's offer yet?"

"No. I have to do some more research on restrictions, and I want to make sure the community will be conservation-friendly."

"These are the cabins you were talking to Jack about?" Bo asked.

"Yes. I'm hoping to put the community near Big Bend."

"Jack's place is near there," Bo said.

"You've got to see Jack's cabin," Krissy said.

"Yeah, I don't know when that might happen."

"You have to see it, Nick," she went on. "It's just terrific. It has everything you're looking for."

"I hope I get to see it soon," Nick said as he turned to focus on his beer bottle.

"Nick, I meant to send you a prospectus on a new project," Krissy said.

He turned to her. "I'm pretty tied up with Big Bend."

Her face grew animated. "This is in Lake Tahoe. A luxury vacation resort on the south shore. A group contacted me, looking for bids from a construction company." She beamed. "Of course, I recommended Stockton."

"Thanks, but I'm not going to take on another project now."

Nick saw Bo take notice as her face fell. An emotion flickered over the guy's face. He cared about her. That was for sure.

"Why don't you send the info over to my father's office." Nick took out his phone and texted her his dad's business contact info. "Tell him you've talked to me and that I think Stockton might be interested."

She glanced at her phone, nodded and tucked it into her purse. "Thanks, Nick. I'll keep you posted."

He waved a hand. "No need. I'm committed to the Big Bend project."

"Your interests are staying in Cloud Canyon?" Bo asked.

Nick simply nodded. He held up the empty to get the bartender's attention.

He cracked open another Bud and set it front of Nick. "Want something to eat?" he asked.

Nick grabbed the one-page menu from a short stack on top of the bar and, after a quick glance, ordered wings and fries. He kept his eyes front but could hear Bo and Krissy starting to softly argue about something or other. Whatever was going on between them wasn't good.

Well, he had his own story going on with Chloe. He didn't have the time or energy to involve himself in the romance between her cousin and the girl who had played a part in helping to split them up six years ago.

***

At nearly ten o'clock, Chloe shut the door to Josh's room. He'd taken forever to fall asleep after the over-excitement of the movie they'd watched, a new Star Wars animated show with lots of fighting and flying. She, however, could hardly keep her eyes open.

Josh had thought he was staying at his grandmother's tonight, and hadn't wanted to leave Grandma's when she'd gone to pick him up. *Thanks, Mom.* She was spared the trouble of coming up with some story about the change in plans, plans she hadn't really made, with the swift decision to order pizza. It was a consolation her little boy was always up for even thought she'd just had pizza last night.

She couldn't help thinking about last night and the meal she'd shared with Nick. And what they'd shared after the pizza was gone. Had Nick gotten her note? Was he angry that she'd sidestepped their dinner plans, no matter how tentative those plans had been? Recalling the kid she'd known in Reno all those years ago, she couldn't think of a time when he'd been angry. Or even upset, for that matter. On that fateful, horrible morning he'd been dazed and apologetic, but that's not the same thing. She didn't think he would be upset tonight.

Being a single mom of an active little boy took her time and her attention. If Nick didn't understand that, she had no hope of their ever coming to an agreement about his involvement in her and Josh's lives. She had to acknowledge that Nick wanted that involvement. He'd been obviously hungry for any information she could give him about their son last night at the inn. A niggle of guilt had struck her that she had never shared news of their baby. Her brother Jack had seemed disapproving when Chloe admitted to him that Nick did want to see Josh and she wasn't going to let him for the time-being. Was she wrong to keep him from Nick? Ugh, it was like her head was going in circles.

She corralled a few of Josh's toys from the floor and straightened the kitchen. Glancing at the clock, she decided she'd put off the inevitable long enough. She had to call Nick and try to explain.

She surveyed the house, hers since right after she'd had Josh. Like the café, it suited her. It had three nice-sized bedrooms and an updated kitchen with a dining area that opened onto a living room. Jack had helped with the remodeling, and the wood floors and wide moldings gave the place a cottage feel. Even with a rowdy little boy in residence, she managed to keep the place in relative order. Furnished in faded vintage fabrics and finds from her mother's antique store, it was clean, neat, and very comfortable.

After smoothing the thick cotton slipcover on the couch for the third time, she settled down and picked up her cell. Nick answered on the second ring.

"Chloe."

She heard it in his voice, his apparent pleasure that she'd called him. His voice was smooth and warm, like him.

"Hi, Nick. Um, I'm sorry tonight didn't work out."

"No problem. I assumed you were busy with Josh."

Neither of them said anything for a long moment. She could hear music playing in the background, along with lots of voices and the clink of glasses.

"Where are you?" she had to ask.

"The Antler."

She snorted. "You're at The Antler?"

He laughed, soft and low. "What, you don't think

it's my kind of place?"

Smooth and polished Nick Stockton in the rough-and-tumble bar seemed too much of a study in contrasts. "Hardly."

"Well, your cousin Bo is here."

"Now, that doesn't surprise me. He practically has his own barstool there."

There was another pause. "He's here with Krissy."

Chloe took a moment to digest that information. Why the heck was Bo with Krissy? "Huh."

"So what do you say about tomorrow night?" Nick asked.

"For dinner?"

"Yeah, dinner." He laughed softly. "For a start."

There was that promise in is voice again. The promise of that passion only he could ever give her. She chewed her bottom lip. Josh was staying with Jack and Laurel tomorrow night and the café was closed on Sundays. She could stay with Nick all night if she wanted to. Did she want to?

The image of Nick in that lovely bed at the Treetop, in that very large tub as well, clinched it for her. He was only here for a short time, which he had admitted himself. She certainly had years to look back on these couple of weeks with the love of her life. She would simply keep her heart out of their affair and indulge herself for once.

"Chloe?"

She blinked and held the phone tighter. "Yes."

"I asked you about dinner."

"And I answered."

"Oh." She could almost picture the grin that curved his mouth. "Good."

"So you're at The Antler, huh?"

"Yeah. I thought we could have dinner here tomorrow night."

She laughed. "No way."

"Not far enough away from prying eyes to keep our secret?"

She smiled. There were only a few people left in Cloud Canyon who didn't know their "secret" by now, anyway. But she caught the teasing tone of his voice.

"Never mind. I think I deserve more than wings and beer for dinner."

"Oh, yeah. You definitely deserve more."

"Um." He sounded uncertain now and she tensed a little bit. "How's Josh tonight?"

Her heart gave a thump but she swallowed and answered him.

"He's finally asleep. He's a ball of energy, that boy."

"My mom use to say the same thing about me."

Once more, silence stretched between them. "Well, I have to open the café in the morning." *Lame.* "So I'll say good night."

"Good night, Chloe. Until tomorrow."

"Good night, Nick."

She disconnected the phone, sinking down into the couch cushions. She'd heard it in his voice. The longing for any information about Josh, yes. But she heard that promise in his voice that she hadn't heard since Reno. For the first time since they'd started this... whatever this was, she'd heard it. The promise of more.

She squeezed her eyes shut and shook her head. No. This was what it was. She'd been a silly young thing when she'd believed his promises, and she doubted she could believe them now.

But wouldn't it be wonderful if she could?

Chapter 12

Nick walked into the crowded café the next morning, up and out of bed earlier than he'd been in a long time. There was something about the air up here, fresh and invigorating, that made him feel like he would be wasting time if he stayed in bed. The constant ticking of the clock on his and Chloe's affair was never far from his mind, either. Whatever the reason, he didn't want to waste a minute of his time in Cloud Canyon.

He let the door close behind him and saw Jack and his wife Laurel seated at one of the tables nearby. Their plates and coffee cups appeared to be empty. Evidently the Butlers weren't the type to sleep in either. Chloe's brother didn't look very welcoming at the moment but Laurel waved and smiled in his direction.

"Hi, Nick."

"Hi." Nick walked over to them. "How are you, Jack?"

Jack grunted in answer but Laurel stuck out her hand. "We haven't met properly. I'm Laurel Butler."

He shook the pretty blonde's hand. "It's very nice to meet you, Laurel."

"Why don't you join us?"

He took another look at Jack. *Uh huh.* There was no way he would willingly sit across the table from that glare. "Thanks, but no." He took a breath. "Jack, I wanted to ask you something."

"Yeah?"

"I wondered if I might be able to take a look at your cabin sometime. Bo and Krissy said it would help give me ideas about Stockton's development."

"Bo and Krissy?" Jack and Laurel asked at the same time.

Nick blinked at their response. "Um, yeah. They said your cabin would be a great example of what I'm looking for with this project. You live over near Big Bend, right?"

"Yeah." Jack appeared to mull over Nick's request. "I guess that would be okay."

Laurel clicked her tongue at Jack's grudging tone and smiled up at Nick. "Come by tomorrow. We don't have anything going in the afternoon."

"That would be great. What time?"

"Laurel…" Jack began.

"How about two o'clock?" Laurel said.

"Sure. Thanks." He looked at Jack again. "Thanks, Jack."

Jack gave a curt nod, obviously eager to get rid of him. Well, Nick didn't need to be told twice. He crossed to the only unoccupied table on the other side of the café and sat.

"I'm ready, Uncle Jack!"

Nick's head shot up and he saw a little boy running from the back of the café toward Jack and Laurel's table. His face was bright, his smile wide, and Nick could only stare as his heart pounded hard and fast. *That's him. That's Josh.*

Chloe's brother looked over at Nick and he could read the concern in the guy's eyes. Jack didn't have to worry about Nick joining them at their table now. He couldn't move if he wanted to. Hell, he could hardly breathe.

"Let's go fishin'," Josh said.

He wore outdoor clothes like his uncle, khaki, denim and flannel with sturdy little hiking boots on his feet. He almost bounced with energy. The little boy apparently hadn't seen Nick, thank God. He would probably wonder why some stranger was gaping at him like a fool.

"Okay, buddy," Jack said. He stood and Josh grabbed on to his hand.

Josh tugged. "Come on, come on."

To Nick it seemed like a regular occurrence, this easy companionship, along with the obvious love his son had for Jack Butler. It was clear that Josh looked up to his uncle, probably the only father figure the kid had. Guilt and jealousy gnawed at Nick's belly. It wasn't his fault. He hadn't known, damn it. Icy cold settled in his chest. He felt cheated all over again by Chloe's decision to keep the kid from him.

"Hey."

He looked up as the redheaded waitress filled the coffee cup in front of him. "Thanks."

She gazed at him, pity clear in her green eyes, and left him alone. Wrapping his hands around the cup, he tried to warm the chill inside. His son was ten feet from him and hadn't spared him a glance. The hard truth struck him straight in his heart then. He was nothing to Josh.

"Nick."

His name was barely a whisper but he heard it. He lifted his head and faced Chloe where she stood, frozen near the back of the café. She looked a little pale and her brow was furrowed. He forced himself to take a long drink of his coffee, unable to speak.

"Bye, Mommy!"

Chloe looked between Nick and their son, then smiled at Josh. "Bye, honey. Have fun."

"Bye, sweetie," Laurel said.

"Bye, Aunt Laurel!" Nick's son called as he tugged Jack out of the café.

Nick watched Jack and Josh leave the café, taking a piece of his heart with them. What would it be like to have Josh look at him like that, like the sun rose and set on him? Would he ever have that with his son?

He finally looked away from the door and found Laurel's gaze on him. There was only sympathy on her face, no censure. Well, it seemed that at least one Butler gave him the benefit of the doubt where Josh was concerned.

Chloe approached his table. "What are you doing here?" She didn't sound angry, just worried. He supposed that was something, anyway. She had no reason to be angry with him. How the hell had he known that Josh would be there this morning?

"Drinking coffee."

She fiddled with the ties of her apron. "Jack takes Josh fishing almost every Saturday."

"Yeah, I remember you saying something about fishing." He shook his head, taking in a deep breath. "But seeing him here? I was a little surprised, is all."

Her brows drew together. "He didn't see you?"

"No." It pissed him off when she breathed a soft sigh. "Jesus, what did you think I was going to do, Chloe? Go up to him and introduce myself?"

"No." She shook her head. "You wouldn't do that to him."

He snorted. At least she had a little faith in him. "I just didn't expect him to be here," he said.

He could see it on her face, the indecision she grappled with. Was she wondering if keeping him from Josh was the right thing to do? Maybe she was beginning to think he deserved a chance to know their son. God, he hoped she came to believe that. But he couldn't push her, not now. Not yet.

"Can I have a western omelet?" he asked.

"Okay." She pulled out the chair opposite and sat, her brows still drawn together. "Are we still on for tonight?"

Despite the morning's tension, there was no question in his mind. "Of course."

"Good. I..." Her gaze strayed to the spot that had been occupied by their son a few minutes ago before turning back to him. "I'm looking forward to it."

Nick drained his coffee and nodded. "So what time do you want me to pick you up?"

She shook her head. "I'll drive over to the inn, if that's okay."

More conditions, then. But he was dancing to her tune at the moment.

"Sure. I've checked out the restaurants in Truckee online and I think The Timbers looks pretty good."

"That's Jack and Laurel's favorite place. I haven't been there in years but it's supposed to be terrific."

"Great. I'll make the reservations."

The bell in the kitchen dinged a few times and the

redhead bustled by with a tray laden with full plates.

Chloe stood. "I should get busy."

"I'll give you call later?"

She smiled at last, the expression almost as bright as their son's had been, and nodded. "I'll get Tom working on your omelet."

She hurried toward the back of the café and Nick toyed with his coffee cup. Had she really been worried that he would do something so foolish as to force himself on their son? In her defense she really didn't know him very well, but he could change that. He had to change the way she thought about him. Make her see that he was worth taking that chance. He was worth having her and their son in his life.

He just had to prove it to her.

***

Chloe dressed for her dinner date with Nick. She'd never had a date with him, not in Reno six years ago and not in the short time he'd been in Cloud Canyon. She chose to wear another creation of Laurel's, the top swirled with blue trimmed in those crystal beads that reminded her of Nick's eyes. She paired it with white Capri pants and strappy sandals. She was going for sexy and chic, and felt that she'd nearly nailed it.

Her hair was down again, loose and shining. Every day she pulled it back in a ponytail for work. It was nice to just be Chloe tonight instead of Chloe Butler, single mom and business owner. She knew how tonight would end: with her in that big bed of Nick's at the Treetop. Would she have the nerve to stay all night? Oh, she wanted to. She had no doubts that he would want her to stay. He seemed to enjoy the afterglow as much as the lovemaking. She longed to give herself up just once to the comfort he offered. It was absolute bliss to stay cuddled in his arms.

The uncertainty of the morning bit into her again. When she'd seen Nick and Josh in the café, no more than ten feet separating the two loves of her life, her heart had skittered to a stop. She hadn't thought for a second that Nick would approach their son. But the longing on his face, the anguish she'd seen in his expression as Josh left with Jack, had cut her deeply. She was wrong to keep Josh from Nick. She knew that now. But how could she manage to bring them together and make sure Josh wouldn't get hurt?

Nick wasn't staying in Cloud Canyon. Heck, he

would probably be gone before the month was out. Should she bring a man into Josh's life who wouldn't stick around?

She stared at herself in the mirror, seeing nothing but a future without Nick. It would hurt her when he left, too. She was able to admit that to herself. But she was an adult. She'd been hurt before and knew that the pain passed with time. But Josh? He had no clue. Every adult in his short life was steadfast and constant.

The subject of his father was never mentioned, not by him or any of her family. But he was getting older. Once he was in Kindergarten the other kids, kids with dads who came to school functions or picked them up from school, would wonder about Josh's dad. And they would ask questions. Kids didn't pull any punches. Maybe if Nick stayed he could be a real father to Josh.

He wouldn't stay with her, though. And she wouldn't push for that. She wasn't a clinging vine who needed a man to feel complete. But if he stayed in Cloud Canyon? Maybe tonight he would tell her more about the project he planned for Stockton. If it wasn't too far from town, and if he would be around now and then to check on things, then maybe letting him get involved with Josh would work. She owed it to Nick and to Josh to see if some kind of arrangement like that would be possible.

She grabbed her purse, locked up and got into her Wrangler. Ten minutes later she was in front of the Treetop Inn. She parked and pulled the brake, taking a breath to steel herself. It was about a half an hour drive to Truckee. Then they would share a leisurely dinner at one of the most beautiful restaurants in the Sierra Nevada. Then more time spent in his room at the Treetop. She would have so much time alone with Nick. Tingles danced over her skin and she welcomed the sweet anticipation.

Decisions tomorrow. Nick tonight.

***

Nick brushed his hair back from his forehead and straightened his collar. Crisp white shirt and pressed chinos, courtesy of the laundry Fred recommended, would suit the occasion. From the photos online The Timbers, with its rustic elegance, looked like the perfect spot for their first real date. Neutral ground, gorgeous setting, delicious food and Chloe. He couldn't ask for more.

A knock sounded at the door and Nick pulled it open to find Chloe framed there. That hair, that face, that body. Wow. From head to toe, this was the woman he'd dreamed about since Reno. The woman he'd only come to want more since she'd let him back into her life—or at least back into her arms

"Hello, gorgeous," he said. "Six o'clock. Right on time."

She flushed that pretty shade of pink and smiled. That gut-punched him again. *Man*. He grabbed his leather jacket and ushered her down the stairs and out of the inn. He opened the passenger door of the Ridgeline and she climbed inside.

"Nice truck," she said.

When he walked around to the driver's side and got in he found her straightening the mess of brochures and papers on the floor at her feet.

She looked up at him and shrugged. "Sorry. I rearrange things."

"No problem." Nick closed his door and started the truck. "My life could use some rearranging."

If she guessed that he meant more in that statement, she didn't give any indication. Nick pulled away from the curb and headed toward US 80. She was quiet beside him on the drive into Truckee, but the silence wasn't awkward. The women he'd dated in the past had always seemed to be talking about themselves or flattering him or trying to lure him into some shallow conversation. Chloe was nothing like them. He'd known that from the first minute he'd met her in Reno, and hadn't realized how much he'd missed that. How much he'd missed her, really.

He pulled into the parking lot of the restaurant. It was a huge thing, with thick timber peaks and rough rock walls.

"Wow," he said "The pictures online hadn't done this place justice."

"It is gorgeous."

"It's contemporary in style yet still captures the raw beauty of the surrounding woods and Truckee River. It's perfect."

He waved her in front of him and they went inside. Linens dressed the tables, balancing the rustic beams ceilings and massive chandeliers made out of antlers. Nick was glad he'd called ahead so they wouldn't have to wait with the dozen or so people in the flagstone entry. They were led to a table tucked right against one of the wide windows with a spectacular view of the river.

"This place has a lot of the elements I'm looking for in Stockton's new project."

Her eyes lit with interest. "You haven't told me much about it."

"Not much to tell, yet. I don't want to jinx it, but the property we're considering would be as perfect as the setting for this restaurant."

She nodded. "I would love to hear more."

"You would?"

A smile curved her lips. "You're invested in this, Nick. I can see your excitement when you talk about it."

"Yeah, it's the first time my father ever gave me the reins on something this big."

"Your father?" she fiddled with her napkin before placing it on her lap. "Are you close to your father?"

He thought about that question. "I guess. He's not a touchy-feely type of dad."

"Ours was. He took us into the Forest, fishing, hiking, whatever. We lost him when I was in middle school."

That gave him pause. There sure was a lot they

didn't know about each other. That was for sure.

"Damn, I'm sorry."

She nodded, and talk kind of stalled after that. The server came by and they ordered their meals. He added a bottle of red to go with the steaks they'd each chosen. The dinner was all he'd expected, steaks done to perfection, accompanied by fresh greens and crisp potatoes and a chocolate soufflé for two neither of them minded waiting to be created just for them. The candlelight and subtle music served to create a coziness despite the soaring ceilings and number of other patrons. Talk soon came easily between them again, focused on the food, the wine, the ambiance. Apparently she didn't want to discuss anything else serious tonight. That suited Nick. For now.

But later… He would have Chloe in his room at the Treetop. They would give each other so much pleasure they would nearly die from it. And afterwards, maybe he would get her to lower that wall of hers and have a real conversation.

About their son, yeah. About what happened in Reno. And about their future. If he'd doubted he wanted her and Josh in his life, after this morning he was sure of it.

He would do his damnedest to prove to her that she and Josh were safe with him.

He wouldn't lose her again.

Chapter 13

Chloe stretched out on the bed, still trembling from the pleasure Nick had given her. He grinned up at her and kissed her belly, coming up to cover her with his body.

"Ah, I love to make you... blush," he rasped.

"Nick," she whispered.

He teased her with his hands, his lips, and when he finally entered her, pulsing deep inside, she felt herself soar as her second orgasm crested. She'd never felt like this. And with the attention he paid her, she could almost imagine she was the only woman in the world for him.

She knew he'd had other lovers, before Reno and after, and no doubt he would have more after Cloud Canyon. But tonight he was just hers. She squeezed her eyes shut and let the pleasure overtake her. He moaned her name as he shuddered deep within her and she felt a connection she'd never experienced before. It was as if he'd held a piece of her all these years and had just given it back.

He collapsed on the pillow beside her, his breath coming fast in her ear. "God, you kill me."

She took a long moment to catch her breath.

Reaching up, she traced a finger over his jaw. "You're a wonderful lover," she breathed.

His brows arched. "Making love with you, Chloe, is like nothing else."

She took his words at their meaning and ducked her head as she blushed again. He was so beautiful, relaxed yet gazing at her with such intensity. She felt the world tremble beneath her for a moment. She had to get back on solid ground. She swallowed and placed her hand on his chest. Mmm. Solid.

"Tell me more about your project, Nick."

He blinked, then shifted to fold his arms behind his head. "It's pretty ambitious, the Big Bend project. The biggest I've ever been involved with for Stockton." He smiled at her. "But I'm up to it."

She could hear the pride in his voice, the thrill of a challenge, and the faith that he could meet it. Who knew Nick had ambitions?

"Jack said something about cabins?" she asked.

"Yes. Luxurious, state-of-the-art cabins. Big and custom built, with all the amenities. Wide plank floors, granite counters, custom cabinetry. High tech and wired for sound and everything else, but with the rustic beauty of the surrounding forest." He gestured as he spoke, and she could almost see what he envisioned. "Oh, and windows. Huge wide windows. I've only visited the Forest a couple of times but the views are spectacular. I think these homeowners will want to bring the outside in as much as possible."

She nodded. "Jack's cabin is a great place to get ideas, then. He's incorporated all the things you've mentioned."

"That's what Bo and Krissy said."

There was that name again. Krissy, the woman who'd put an end to them six years ago. But it didn't hurt to hear it tonight, spoken so plainly. Why she was at The Antler with Bo last night was beyond Chloe but she couldn't care less at the moment.

"Vacation homes, then?"

"Not really, no. The owners might choose to use theirs only for vacations but I'm planning on the project becoming a community of custom cabins. Outfitted for year-round living. They'll be restrictions on leases, as well."

"So these will be pretty big, right?"

"Yes. Family homes. I want people to put down roots here."

Family. Her breath caught. He was Josh's family. Would he want to put roots down here, too? Did she want him to? She could only nod as he went on.

"The area, Cloud Canyon especially, seems terrific," he went on. "How are the schools?"

"The schools?"

"Yeah. I know Josh isn't in Kindergarten yet, but you and Jack grew up here."

"Oh, Yuma County has great schools."

"Good. Another selling point."

Schools, community, roots. This wasn't the Nick she'd thought she knew. He seemed grounded, committed and focused.

"I think you've chosen a great location. Big Bend is beautiful."

"Yeah." He gently rubbed her shoulder, her back, as she stroked his chest. "I want to see more of the Forest, though. Do you hike?"

She smiled. "Of course."

"We should go tomorrow." He brushed a thick strand of hair from her cheek and tucked it behind her ear. "What do you say?"

Her mind worked. Josh would be at Jack and Laurel's until the afternoon. "Why not?"

"Good."

"I'd have to go home and get my stuff."

"I guess you can go." His eye sparkled. "In the morning, Chloe."

She caught his meaning and thought to tease him. "I thought you wanted to hike? That means an early start."

"I want you to stay here with me tonight." He drew her closer. "All night."

So much temptation in his voice, smooth and honey sweet. She couldn't resist. "If you insist."

He dropped a tender kiss on her lips. "Besides, ever since I've been here I can't stay in bed much after sunrise. Must be the air."

"Not usually an early riser?"

He laughed. "Hardly. My mother says she used to have to stop just short of dynamite to get me out of bed for school."

"So you're close to your mom, too?"

"Yeah. She's great. You?"

"My mom is wonderful, and not just with Josh. She runs her own business, too."

"It must be a Butler thing."

She grinned. "Yep."

"I do like getting a jump on the day here, though. And that gives me more time to spend with you."

That could be a well-rehearsed line but he looked so sincere. Like before as they'd made love, she felt his focus completely on her. She'd never felt that, not before Reno and not after. Only with Nick.

She kissed him and in an instant they were lost in the passion that had shaken them both just a few minutes earlier. And afterwards she didn't hesitate to cuddle back into his arms. Even though her mind thought it was foolish, her heart wanted to lose itself with him.

If only for tonight.

***

"You shouldn't have done that, Laurel."

Laurel just shook her head and gazed at Jack. His Butler-blue eyes were intent and his brows were drawn together. She stretched out beside him in their big bed and propped her chin on his chest. "You know I'm right, Jack. Deal with it."

He grunted. "Josh will still be here tomorrow at two. Hell, Chloe will probably be here, too."

She shrugged. "What better time to acquaint Nick with his son? And with Josh's mom looking on?"

Jack let out a breath. "My sister's going to be pretty pissed. She doesn't like to be blindsided."

"You stubborn Butlers don't scare me," she teased. She suddenly sobered. "Come on, Jack. You saw the look on Nick's face this morning. There's no denying what he was feeling. He looked almost hungry to know his little boy."

"No. I saw that for sure." She quirked an eyebrow at him so he elaborated. "If I'd seen my son for the first time? I don't know if I could have stayed there and let us just walk out the door."

"Well, I'm willing to risk Chloe's wrath tomorrow. Nick deserves to meet Josh."

Jack was quiet, a natural state for him. Then he gave a reluctant nod. "Yeah. I can't believe he was able to control himself like that."

"I think he's just being careful. He doesn't want to spook your sister."

"So you think he wants more than just a fling?"

"I do." She kissed him and settled down once more. "Jeez, I can't believe I'm turning into one of you."

"Into one of what?"

"A Butler. Meddling in the lives of people I love."

Jack grabbed her up and turned until she was pinned beneath him. "Ah, honey. You were a Butler the minute I found you on the side of the road."

She laughed and gave herself up to him again.

***

Nick woke after the best night's sleep he'd had in years. Chloe was all soft and warm in his arms, her head tucked against his chest the way he liked. He ran his fingers through her incredible hair and breathed in. Mmm. Flowers and cinnamon.

She couldn't seem to stop touching him, not while they made love and not after as they'd talked about the project. Even in sleep he could feel her tentative touch on his chest, his arm, his face.

He'd forgotten the little sounds she made while sleeping, soft sighs and murmurs. They hadn't spent the whole night together since Reno, but there was no mistaking this woman in his arms as any other. This was the mother of his child. His Chloe.

Today they would spend the day together—or as long as she gave him today. At least she would show him her favorite parts of the Forest. That alone was worth the price of admission. He knew the cost, though. He couldn't push her on her decision about Josh. He would pay that fee for now. Hopefully soon she would trust him enough to let him at least meet the little boy. God, when he'd seen him at the café he could barely catch his breath. He was beautiful, made with bits of her and bits of him. He was perfect.

Chloe let out another sigh and cuddled closer. His body reacted and he rolled over to wake her with kisses and more. Her skin, her hair, her scent... God, it was like he could never get enough of her. He grabbed another condom from the nightstand and gave in to her. She fit him perfectly, and they moved together until the pressure became too much. He caught her cries in his mouth as she climaxed, letting go in the next instant.

When they finally untangled themselves, the sun was just beginning to peek through the windows.

He grinned down at her. "What a way to wake up."

"Hmm." She stroked his arms, his chest. "Still up for that hike?"

"You think you wore me out?" He laughed. "Close, but I'm still up for it."

She blushed and smiled at the same time.

"God, I love it when you look at me like that."

They rose and showered together then dressed. He wore jeans and one of the flannel shirts he'd bought in town with his new hiking boots. He glanced over and saw she hesitated after she slipped those cute little pants she'd worn last night up over her lovely legs. Something was up, and he was almost afraid to ask her what it was.

"We have to go by my place to pick up my stuff," she said.

He sensed her apprehension and guessed its cause. She was going to let him see where she lived with their son. He tied his boots and sought to skirt the subject. "Do you have a pack I can borrow?"

She paused again, and then nodded. They finished

dressing and walked outside into another beautiful summer day in the mountains. Crisp, bright, and with the promise of warmth later in the day. And that blue, blue sky. He could get used to Cloud Canyon.

He followed her Jeep in his truck, finally pulling to stop in front a snug little house not far from the center of Cloud Canyon. It was one-story done in clapboard, and it was neat and fresh-looking with window boxes and a wide covered porch. It had a steeply-pitched roof which he guessed helped with the heavy snowfalls half the year. The property had a well-tended lawn, a garage set back and a line of tall trees behind it. He would have had a hard time imagining a better place to raise their son.

He stepped up onto the porch beside her. There were thoughtful touches here too, comfortable wicker chairs with worn cushions and a swing attached to the porch ceiling. Had she rocked their son in that swing when he was a baby? Did they sit and look out at the stars now, or maybe count fireflies? God, he'd missed so much of his son's life. Of the life they could have had together all these years. Anger and frustration threatened, and he consciously set it aside with more than a little bit of effort.

She stilled again at the front door. He forced himself to remain unaffected, but it nearly killed him. She finally unlocked the door and he stepped in behind her.

The house was furnished a lot like the little apartment above the café, clean and crisp yet comfortable. Toys in bins lined one wall of the living room and he stopped himself from pawing through them to learn a little about what his son favored. He spotted Legos, action figures, some play tools and dinosaurs. Everything screamed "boy" and Nick's lips twitched in a smile.

"I like your house."

She smiled. "Thanks."

"You've made a very nice home for our son. For Josh," he quickly amended.

She nodded. "Have a seat and I'll go get ready."

He ran his damp palms over his jeans and forced himself to relax. This hit him harder than he'd anticipated. She lived here with their son. Bedtime stories, bath time, meals together. The list of things he'd missed grew longer.

He sat on the couch and looked around. The house, like the café, bore Chloe's stamp. There was comfortable worn furniture in good condition, and everything was neat and orderly, aside from the jumble of toys. But even they were contained in their bins.

She straightened and rearranged things all the time, especially when she was nervous. Chairs, napkins, the papers in his truck. He hadn't noticed that in Reno, but they'd been little more than kids then. Maybe this was something she'd developed after she had Josh. Order and routine was important to a kid. His mom had made sure that Nick had that, especially with the long hours his father had worked when Nick was little.

In Chloe's house everything had a place and was neatly tucked into it. Did he even have a place here? Well, he hadn't been kidding when he'd told her his life could use some order. He shifted and felt something jab his leg from between the cushions. He reached down, withdrew a small plastic action figure and smiled. Boba Fett. He ran his fingers over the plastic, his chest tight as he imagined Josh playing with the figure.

"Okay, I'm ready."

Nick looked over at Chloe. Her hair was pulled back in a ponytail and she wore a pink T-shirt with khaki shorts and hiking boots. She looked fresh and hot, and he felt that rush of attraction again. That connection. This was right. *She* was right.

"Oh, sorry about that." Chloe gestured toward the action figure in his hand. "Sometimes I miss one."

Nick held it up. "Boba Fett. I loved Star Wars when I was a kid."

A tender expression crossed her face. "It's Josh's favorite."

Warmth bloomed in his chest. "We have something in common, then."

He handed her the toy and she tossed it in one of the bins. "You have more than that in common, Nick." She sat down beside him, her shoulders finally losing that rigidity he'd noticed since they'd gotten dressed this morning. "You saw him yesterday. He's you all over. Even more than in the pictures you saw."

The pain struck him again, loss and anger mixing with regret. "I know."

They were quiet there in the home she'd made for their son. The home she'd made without him. Suddenly the air seemed too thick.

He stood. "How about we hit the trail?"

She nodded and he looked at her again. Her gaze was soft, her eyes wet, and he dared to think she was softening toward him. Her body was his, there was no question after last night. He hid his smile. And this morning. But her heart?

Suddenly, he wanted that more than anything. He knew she would never give it halfway, either. Nope. When he won her heart, he would have all of her. And just maybe everything he'd ever wanted. Her trust, her love and their son.

Chapter 14

Nick hiked back down the mountain behind Chloe, exhausted and exhilarated at the same time. He'd suspected his visits to the Forest had only been the tip of the iceberg and today confirmed it. Chloe had shown him spots he would never have found on his own, hidden trials with towering Jefferson Pine trees and so many wildflowers whose names she'd told him and he'd already forgotten. It was clear that she loved the area. It was as big a part of her as it must be for her Forest Ranger brother.

"Do you hike with Jack?"

"Sometimes. Jeanine comes with me once in a while."

"Jeanine?"

"She works for me."

"Oh, the redhead?"

She nodded as they came to where he'd parked the Ridgeline. "Jack spends a lot more time in these woods than I ever could."

"You work every day the café's open?"

"Yep. It's mine and I guess I don't trust anyone else to run things like I do."

He more than suspected that there was a lot in that statement she wasn't saying. Well, he wouldn't push her about her life and how he apparently had no part in it. Not while they were in this pleasant little bubble in the woods.

They got in the truck but before starting it he turned to her. "What are you doing later?"

Her brows arched then she shook her head. "I have to get Josh in a little while. We usually have dinner at my mom's on Sunday night."

"Maybe we could grab lunch?"

She chewed her lower lip. "Nick, last night was wonderful." Her eyes sparkled at him. "And this morning. But I don't have the freedom to do whatever I want."

"Then you do want to hang out with me." He had to smile. "And not just in bed?"

"Yes." Her eyes suddenly flashed at him. "All right? Yes. But I can't."

"Because of Josh." He blew out a breath. "Because of our son. Don't you see how screwed up that is?"

She gaped at him and he nearly bit his tongue. God, he'd done it now.

"Nick, I... I have to do some more thinking about

this. About everything."

Hope flared within him. "So you *are* thinking about letting me see Josh?"

She blinked at him. "How could I not? But please. Just give me some time?"

He grinned. He couldn't help it. "Baby, take all the time you need. I'm just so damn happy you're thinking about it."

He kissed her and after a brief hesitation she wrapped her arms around him. If Chloe let him see Josh, let him get to know their son, he would finally have the chance to prove to her that he was just what they needed.

And that he was smart enough to know they were everything he'd never known he'd always wanted.

***

Chloe stepped out of the shower and glanced at her watch set on the vanity. One thirty. Jack and Laurel would be expecting her soon. After Nick had driven her back to her house she couldn't seem to let go of him. His kisses in his truck, hot and sweet and promising so much more than they'd shared in the past, both thrilled her and scared the heck out of her. She walked into her room, put on jeans and a fresh T-shirt and pulled her hair back with a hair band. After slipping on her Keds, she did a quick sweep of the house. Everything looked to be in order. Her gaze fell on the couch. Oh, what she and Nick had done on that couch after their hike! She should have just gone inside alone. She should have let him go with no more than another delicious kiss, but she couldn't. She hadn't been lying when she said her time wasn't her own. But she'd wanted to extend their time together as much as he apparently did. Oh, this was dangerous.

She grabbed her purse and headed over to Jack and Laurel's. Getting out of the Wrangler, she stopped a moment to look at the cabin. It was rustic and pretty at the same time, fitting in perfectly with its surroundings. Yet she knew Jack had outfitted the place with everything Nick had said he wanted to bring to his Big Bend project. Maybe she could talk Jack into letting Nick see the cabin. She was considering letting Nick be a part of Josh's life, after all. If that happened, her big brother was going to have to learn to play nice with him. She snorted. *Boys.*

She walked up to the front door and knocked. Laurel pulled it open, a smile on her face. "Hi, Chloe."

"Hi." She hugged Laurel. "Was Josh a good boy?"

"As always." Laurel closed the door and turned. "We're outside. Come on."

Chloe followed her out onto the deck. Once more, the gorgeous view struck her. Jack's yard stretched back toward a copse of trees, with a large clearing for his dog Smokey to run around. Josh was playing with Smokey, wearing a big grin as he tossed a ragged tennis ball for the dog. The shaggy Shepherd mix loved the boy almost as much as he did Jack, jumping up now and then to lick his face. Josh tumbled to ground laughing and Chloe smiled in response.

"He's going to sleep like a rock tonight." Laurel faced her. "And how did you sleep last night?"

"Laurel, stop. You know I was with Nick." She flushed. "Does Jack?"

Laurel shrugged. "Jack's a smart guy. Besides, when we first got together we didn't want to waste any of the time we had."

"I told you. We're not you and Jack. Far from it."

"No." Laurel tilted her head toward the little boy running and laughing in the yard. "You're more."

Were they? Chloe had nothing to say to that, so afraid to even hope that was true.

"Hey, sis." Jack made his way past them out onto the deck, a big plate piled with ribs held in his hands. "Staying for dinner?"

"I should get going. Mom likes us to join her on Sundays."

Jack glanced at Laurel and shrugged. "I tried." He went out onto the deck.

"Look, we have a lot of food," Laurel said. "Your mom won't mind. Stay. We just love having Josh around. And he's having so much fun."

Chloe laughed. "Ooh, dirty pool. Okay. I can't say no to Jack's ribs."

Her brother muttered something she missed as Laurel joined him out on the deck. She went back inside and texted her mom about dinner, and then put her purse down on one of the stools near the granite island. She just turned to rejoin Jack and Laurel when a knock came at the front door.

"Someone's at the door," she called.

More muttering along with Laurel's whispered

admonishments came from outside. What was up with those two?

Laurel came in and hurried to the front door. "Don't be mad."

Chloe stilled. "Laurel, what did you do?"

She pulled the door open and there stood Nick. "Hi, Nick."

"Hi, Laurel." He stepped inside. "Thanks again for inviting me over. I know that Jack wasn't too happy about it." He froze and stared at her. "Chloe?"

Chloe stared back at him for a long moment. *Oh, God.* Josh's laughter reached her, and she saw Nick react. He stiffened, surprise clear in his expression, along with what she could only call cautious excitement.

"He's here," Nick said, his voice low.

Laurel nodded as she shut the door, a blush staining her cheeks. "Jack and I thought today would be as good a time as any for you to see the cabin, Nick." She had the grace to look embarrassed, at least. "I guess I forgot to mention we were watching Josh."

Chloe couldn't make herself move. Before she could think of what to say, she heard Josh's footsteps pounding on the deck right before he ran into the house.

"Mommy! Uncle Jack said we can stay for ribs. I thought we were eating at Grandma's." He skidded to a stop and looked up at Nick. "Oh. Hi."

For one heart-stopping moment Chloe thought she would faint for the first time in her life. *Breathe, Chloe.* She glanced over and saw Laurel holding herself very still.

"Hi." Nick walked over to Josh and crouched down to his level. "I'm Nick. I'm a friend of your mommy's."

Josh looked from him to her and back again. He seemed to weigh Nick's words, finally taking them at face value. "What's your name again?"

"Nick."

Josh stared at him a little longer, and then turned to Chloe. "So can we stay for ribs?"

She let out her breath at last. "Sure, honey."

Josh looked back at Nick. "Are you gonna stay?"

"I…" He looked at Chloe.

She couldn't send him away. Not with such hope clear on his face. "Yes, Nick's staying."

"Cool. Come out and play with me and Smokey if you want."

Then Josh ran back outside, calling loudly for the dog. Laurel followed him outside and shut the door leading to the deck, giving them some privacy.

"I gotta sit down." Nick sank down onto the leather couch. "I had no idea he would be here, Chloe. You have to believe me."

"I know." She sat beside him. "This was all Jack and Laurel's doing."

He ran his gaze over her face. "So you're okay with this?"

"Yes." She placed her hand on his arm. "Thanks for not telling him."

"It's not my place." He ran his hands over his thighs, his body stiff. "Will I ever get used to it?"

"Use to what?"

"That connection. That, that… Man, I look into his face and it's just… there."

"I know. I felt it the minute I held him for the first time."

"I wish…" He had a faraway look in his gorgeous crystal blue eyes. "Ah, never mind."

"Come on." She stood, blinking away the sudden

tears. "Let's get Jack to give you that tour you wanted while the ribs cook."

Nick stood and smiled, his body losing some of that tension. "Thanks."

They set aside talk of regrets and might-have-beens as they went back outside.

***

Nick took mental notes as Jack showed him around the cabin. It had all he was looking for, and new designs and layouts for the project were coming to him fast. He would have no problem making up some preliminary sketches when he went back to the inn tonight.

Jack stepped out onto the deck and Nick followed. Laurel handed him a bottle of beer and Nick settled into one of the Adirondack chairs. Aside from the grill there was little else on the deck but a few of these chairs. It was obvious they didn't eat out here. That made sense, being so close to the woods. No need to attract wildlife up to the house. That was good to keep in mind for the project, too.

He gazed out at the woods and mountains in the distance, the colors taking his breath. "Man, what a view."

Laurel nodded. "It was what struck me when I

stayed here with Jack that first time."

"Jeez, how could you ever leave?"

She laughed. "I couldn't."

He smiled and drank some of his beer. He caught sight of Chloe talking to Josh down in the yard, plucking grass and leaves out of his hair and brushing off his shirt. The little boy squirmed as she ran her fingers through his hair and Nick was struck with recognition. That was the move she'd made toward him that first night at the inn. It had been intimate and affectionate, and even now it caused his blood to heat. Love and passion. That was his Chloe.

"Ribs are ready," Jack called.

Nick stood. "Anything I can do?"

"Nope. Just head on into the house."

Nick went into the dining area off the kitchen and sat. He fiddled with his silverware as the Butlers brought the food to the table. There was a tension hanging in the air, from both Jack and Laurel. Nick knew for certain that this was some sort of test and he would be damned if he failed it.

Chloe must have taken Josh to get cleaned up, because his face looked freshly-scrubbed and shiny when he climbed up onto the chair across from him.

"Oh boy, I love Uncle Jack's ribs."

"They look great," Nick said.

"Yeah. We don't eat here much, just at Grandma's and Aunt Beth's."

Chloe glanced over at Nick as she served Josh. "Bo's mother."

He nodded. As they ate, talking about everything and anything, Nick could hardly take his eyes off his son. Josh was all boy, from the smear of barbeque sauce on his face to wiping his hands on his shirt despite the napkin Chloe had tied around his neck.

"You'll need a good dunking tonight, boy," Chloe said.

Josh waved his little hand. "How do you know Mommy, Nick?"

Nick set down his fork. "From a long time ago."

"So, you were friends?"

"Yep."

"And now?"

"Still friends." He glanced over at Chloe, who watched him closely. "At least, I hope so."

Josh nodded. "I was friends with Will last summer but then we weren't cuz he went to live with his dad." He drank some of his chocolate milk, getting a mustache he tried to lick off. "But he came back to Pre-K after Christmas and we're friends again."

"That's good, right?" Nick asked.

"Yep. Until his dad takes him again. When will that be, Mommy?"

"I think Will's parents share custody, sweetie. That means they take turns having him live with them. I don't know exactly when Will's dad takes him."

"I'm glad I don't have a dad to take me away."

Nick stilled, then nodded. "Yeah. I think if you had a dad he would never take you away from your mom."

Josh stared at him. "Nope."

Chloe shot him a grateful look and he felt the cloud of tension lift a bit. After dinner he thanked Jack and Laurel for everything and made a hasty exit. Josh had waved goodbye to him and it had nearly broken his heart.

Was he the fool to hope for more? Well, he had to be since he sure as hell did. He hoped that someday soon he would never have to say goodbye to them again.

Chapter 15

By Tuesday afternoon Nick seemed to have all his ducks in a row regarding the Big Bend project. Sunday night, after taking long minutes to savor every memory he had of his time with Josh, he'd sketched out some cabin designs. He'd emailed them to his father on Monday and heard back from him right away. Joe was excited about Big Bend, from Nick's selection of the land to the designs to the entire concept. When he'd called, Nick had nearly told him about Josh. Meeting the little boy, talking to him, had been incredible. But he couldn't get his parents' hopes up. It was bad enough that his own were hung up in the air as high as the Sierra Nevada.

His phone trilled and he looked at the display and answered. "Speak of the devil. Hi, Dad."

"Hey, son. I just wanted to bring you up to speed."

"About what?"

"The realtor contacted me a few days ago, Nick. Kelly something. About the Lake Tahoe project."

"I didn't know that. You saw what I sent you on it?"

"Yeah, and I want you to pursue this."

"Sure. I'd be happy to."

"In fact, why don't you put the Big Bend project on the backburner for now?"

"No." His answer was sharper than he'd intended. "I'm focused on this project, Dad."

"Look, this is a bigger deal. Maybe you can set Big Bend aside until this is settled."

"I'm sorry, but no. I'll make the offer for Stockton if you like, but then I'm out of it."

Joe was quiet for a second. "What is it with you and Big Bend?"

He thought for a second. He couldn't talk about Josh to his father. Not yet.

"I'm invested in this project," he finally said. "You'll have to let Stockton's team work on Lake Tahoe. My focus is on Big Bend and that's where it's staying."

His father was quiet on the other end, and Nick worried that he would pull him out of Big Bend.

"All right," his father said. "Nick, I've never heard you so excited about a project."

Relief nearly made Nick's limbs weak. "I think this can be spectacular, Dad. I went hiking in the Forest and the views? I want to make sure we offer our homeowners at least a taste of that."

"You went hiking?"

"Yes."

Joe chuckled. "You are turning into a mountain man. That's what your mother said when I told her you were going on about the springs and the Truckee River."

"I bet Mom was surprised."

"She said you haven't played outside so much since you were a kid."

It was on the tip of his tongue again, the news about Josh. He could still picture him how he had looked at Jack's cabin, rolling around in the backyard with that shaggy dog. How would they react? Shock? Disapproval? Excitement? He had no idea.

"So are you staying in Cloud Canyon?" his father asked.

"Yeah."

"For how long?"

Forever. "For as long as it takes." His father couldn't know the true import of his words, but he sure meant them. He was staying in Cloud Canyon until he figured out how to have Chloe and Josh in his life. Hell, maybe he would never leave.

"Hmm." His father was quiet again, which meant those wheels were turning. "Well, keep me posted and I'll let you know what's up with Tahoe."

"Sounds good."

"See ya', son."

"Bye, Dad."

Joe might have put aside his arguments for now, but Nick knew he'd bring it up again and soon. His father was nothing if not persistent. Nick was a little bit frustrated, but only with himself. He'd missed seeing Chloe Monday night, too. He'd wanted to talk to her after that dinner at Jack's cabin, but he'd been so tied up with Stockton business yesterday he'd missed his chance.

After making Stockton's offer at Kelly's office later than morning, he swung by the café. He pulled the truck to a stop and stepped out. He'd gotten some great news about the Big Bend project and couldn't wait to share it with Chloe. If that didn't tell him they were more than bedmates, he didn't know what would. Would she believe it, though?

"Hello!" a female voice called.

Nick looked a few storefronts ahead and saw a

woman waving at him from an open door. He waved a hand and walked toward her. "Hello."

The woman, maybe in her early fifties, flashed a smile at him. There was no mistaking her identity as he got closer. This was obviously Chloe's mother. Aside from the eyes, the resemblance was striking.

She held out her hand. "You must be Nick."

Uh oh. What did she know about him? "Yes." He shook her hand. "Mrs. Butler?"

She laughed, and the sound was very much like Chloe's. "Is it that obvious?"

He gave her his best Stockton smile. "It's clear where Chloe got her beauty."

She winked at him. "Oh, Jeanine was right. You are a charmer."

He looked at the storefront behind her and at the crowded, attractive window. "Is this your antique store?"

"Yes. And Bo's mom owns this strip along with the boutique down at the other end." She gestured toward the stores in between. "There's Chloe's café, and Laurel's studio and gallery is just down a ways, too."

He glanced down the tidy row of storefronts. "Lots

of Butlers."

He looked back to find her studying him and he could guess she saw Josh in his features. That would explain the affection in her gaze, along with the open speculation.

"I was just going to the café for a late lunch," he said.

"Come to dinner tonight, Nick."

"Um, I don't think that's a good idea."

"Tuesday night is Butler dinner night at my sister-in-law's. Bo's mom. You know Bo. Jack and Laurel will be there, as always. And Chloe and Josh."

Nick thought for a moment. "Maybe I should ask Chloe."

Mrs. Butler waved a hand. "Chloe won't mind. I heard you all had a lovely dinner over at Jack and Laurel's on Sunday."

Whoa. He had to be careful around these Butlers. Their heavy-handed matchmaking would only scare Chloe for sure. "Well, I appreciate the offer."

She looked crestfallen and he found he couldn't stand to see that look on her face any more than he could on Chloe's. "All right. I'd love to. Thank you, Mrs. Butler."

She smiled at him again and he had the distinct impression that he'd stepped right into her trap. "See you at seven, Nick."

He nodded. At least he would get to see Chloe and Josh for dinner. He stilled for a moment. Maybe. He'd better square it with Chloe before she found out from some Butler.

***

The café was nearly empty by the time Jack came for his usual late lunch. The bell above the door rang and Chloe turned. "Like clockwork."

"Huh?"

She spun to find Nick standing there. "I thought you were Jack. This is his usual lunch time."

Nick let the door close. "Disappointed?"

She felt that rush of warmth and welcomed it. "No." He sat down and she joined him at his table. "You've been busy."

"Did you miss me?" he asked.

"Yes."

His eyes sparkled. "I missed you last night."

She straightened the napkin in front of her, lining up the edges as she took a breath. "Are you busy tonight?"

"Funny you should ask."

"Why?"

"It seems I've been invited to dinner."

She stared at him for a beat and then it hit her. She blew out a breath. "Darn Laurel, anyway."

He chuckled. "Nope. Butler, yes. Laurel, no."

"Then, who?" It struck her, one of the other Butlers in the shopping center. The most meddlesome, in her opinion. "Oh. My mom."

"Yep. I told her I wanted to check with you but she assured me you'd be okay with it."

"I'm sure she did."

"Are you? Okay with it?"

That hopeful expression was on his face again, along with a wariness she hated to see. Had she been being that big of a witch, with her rules about Josh? "Yes, Nick. Come to dinner at my aunt's."

His smile flashed bright. "Thanks." He laughed then. "Your mother's a tough one to say 'no' to."

"Yeah." She stood and tucked the chair back in so

that it was now even with the one beside it. "Karma's a real pain in the butt."

"Why?"

"I did the same thing to Jack and Laurel last year."

Nick raised a brow, then nodded. "Yeah, I could tell she was matchmaking."

"I'm sorry, Nick. I don't want any matchmaking, believe me."

He held up his hands. "All I did was say 'yes' to dinner, Chloe. Don't go thinking I'm orchestrating anything."

"I don't think that."

For a moment she wondered what it would be like for Nick to want to stay. To make a match with her. The only thing she knew for certain was that he wanted to be part of Josh's life. No mention was ever made of being a part of hers. Was he worried about her rejection? Well, she hadn't given him anything, aside from her body. Maybe he was right to be gun shy.

"Did she warn you that all the Butlers will be there?" she asked.

"Yep."

She covered his hand with hers and let out a little laugh. "Good luck."

He turned his hand in her grasp and brought her fingers to his lips. "You'll be there." He kissed her skin. "That's all the luck I need."

She couldn't help but smile at him.

***

Chloe parked her Jeep behind Nick's truck in front of Aunt Beth's house and turned off the ignition. When Josh unbuckled his seatbelt and reached for the door handle. she placed a hand on his arm. "Wait a sec, honey."

He turned to face her. "What?"

"I wanted to let you know that Mommy's friend Nick will be at dinner tonight."

"Oh." Josh gazed through the windshield. "Is that his truck?"

"Yes."

"It's big."

He looked back at her, waiting for her to say something, until he finally blew out a breath. "Come on!"

"Okay, go."

He jumped down from the Jeep and ran up to the

front door. She slowly followed. What would her dear cousin Bo say? He had a knack for hitting the nail on the head. And what about her mother? She already suspected Chloe was seeing Nick, and she'd deflected questions about Sunday night spent at Jack and Laurel's both yesterday and today. Jack had seemed more accommodating at the cabin, though. And it was no secret that Laurel wanted them together. Jeez, how would Nick react to a roomful of Butlers?

Josh knocked on the door and squeezed past Bo when he opened it. "Hey, buddy." Bo looked at Chloe. "Hey, cuz."

Chloe met his gaze. "I know he's here."

"He's being grilled by my mother right now." Bo grinned. "You better go save him."

She left Bo to close the door and walked into the dining room. All eyes were soon on her and she swallowed. Josh sat next to Nick, who was talking around a mouthful of bread.

Nick nodded at something the little boy said, a serious look on his face. "Well, I never watched Clone Wars, but I bet it's pretty good."

"You hafta come over and watch with me." Josh looked over at Chloe. "Mommy, can Nick come over and watch Clone Wars with me?"

"I…" Again, everyone stared at her. Laurel wore an expression of expectation, of blatant encouragement, as did her mom and aunt. Nick's face was bright with obvious hope. Bo wouldn't meet her gaze but even Jack watched warily for her answer. Did they all think she was really such a bitch?

"Of course he can, honey."

"Tonight, Nick." Josh drank his milk and wiped his mouth with his hand. "After dinner."

"Not tonight," her mother said. She looked at Chloe, her gaze thoughtful. "You're coming over to Grandma's for a while tonight, Josh."

Josh's brow furrowed, then he shrugged. "Oh. Tomorrow okay, Nick?"

"Definitely." Nick threw a grateful look in Chloe's direction. "Thanks."

Chloe sent her mother a look of understanding. Tonight, Josh would be occupied and she could spend some time alone with Nick. And apparently Nick was going to spend some time with Josh tomorrow. That sobered her. She wasn't even sure how she felt about it, but her family seemed to think it would be okay.

Her gaze fell on her little boy, oblivious to the undercurrent swirling around him. She prayed it would be okay. From everything she'd learned from Nick since he'd been here, she knew that he would put their son's feelings before anything he himself might be experiencing.

"Check the grill, will you Bo?" her aunt asked.

"Sure thing."

Bo left the table and Chloe finally sat. Jack's brows were arched but Chloe didn't miss the smug smile on Laurel's face. Fine, then. Nick could have some contact with Josh. She wasn't going to tell Josh who he was, though. Not yet.

When Bo returned from the grill, he carried a platter of her aunt's apple-stuffed pork chops. Conversation dwindled as they all began to eat, but as the meal reached its end it picked back up just like Chloe had suspected it would.

"So tell us about your project, Nick," Chloe's mother said. "Jack mentioned cabins?"

Chloe glanced at her brother, who nodded. Amazingly, he seemed to be on board with the rest of the Butlers. Nick smiled his gorgeous grin and began to describe his vision for the Big Bend project. Chloe watched Josh as Nick spoke, seeing interest and a touch of confusion on his face. Did Josh sense a connection? If he could see himself sitting next to Nick, there would be no question that they were father and son.

"That's pretty impressive," Laurel said. "So, like Jack's cabin but bigger?"

Bo laughed. "Bigger isn't always better, cuz."

"Bo," his mother chuckled.

"I'm hoping people will put down roots here near Big Bend." Nick folded his napkin and set it beside his plate, his enthusiasm clear. "Either relocating from the surrounding areas or coming from someplace else." He gazed at Chloe. "I know the more time I spend here the less I want to leave."

She flushed and quickly stood, and then headed into the kitchen. Wrapping her arms around herself, she closed her eyes. Did Nick really want to stay in Cloud Canyon? Indefinitely? She wished she could believe that. It was just too much to hope for, but it was the secret dream she'd held onto since he'd walked into the café that first afternoon.

"Hey," Laurel said softly.

Chloe turned to find Laurel standing there. Glancing behind her, she saw no other Butlers were in earshot. She relaxed a bit and let her arms drop to her sides. "Hey."

"I still can't get over it, Chloe." Laurel stepped closer to her. "To see them side-by-side? Sheesh."

"I know." Chloe blew a hair out of her face and sighed. "And now he's going to come over to watch a show with Josh. Tomorrow."

Laurel was quiet for a moment. "I think it's good that Josh is so young. He takes things at face value."

"I know I have to tell him, Laurel. And sometime soon." Chloe chewed her bottom lip. "I just don't know how he'll react."

Laurel placed her hand on Chloe's arm. "Let him get to know Nick a little better. You don't have to rush into anything."

"But what about my, you know. What I'm doing with Nick?"

"What about it?" Laurel's eyes narrowed. "You told

me you were keeping your heart out of it."

She nodded and tried to look impassive but when Laurel laughed softly, she knew she'd lost. "Okay. I admit it."

Laurel leaned closer. "Admit what?" she urged.

"I'm falling for him again. Oh, what a relief to say it out loud." She held up one hand. "But I'm not a fool, Laurel. I know this is just for now."

Laurel's brow quirked. "Maybe."

"Not maybe. Definitely. But I know Josh has to have some sort of contact with his father. They both deserve that."

Laurel hugged her and Chloe sagged a little against her. "You're a good mother. You'll do what's best for your little boy."

Chloe's throat tightened and she found that she couldn't say anything more, not without bursting into tears there in her aunt's kitchen. Oh, she was fool to let her heart want more. Josh and Nick did both deserve the chance to get to know each other. She could tell Nick was already half in love with their son. That was clear in every expression. It wouldn't take much for Josh to love him back. She was more than halfway there, herself.

That was how it should be. She would just have to make sure that Nick never found out how she really felt about him. She was falling in love with him all over again.

Chapter 16

After dinner was finished, Chloe stood and started picking up the dishes. Nick rose to help her, stilling as all heads turned toward him. "Let me help." He smiled. "It's the least I can do."

"There's a gentleman," Chloe's mother said.

Chloe rolled her eyes and went into the kitchen as Nick bit back a grin. He grabbed the remaining dishes and followed her. He found her standing at the sink, her back to him as she gripped the edge.

"Why is this so hard?" he heard her whisper.

He crossed to stand beside her. "It's family. It's never easy."

"That's not what I mean." She slid her gaze toward him. "You've been just great with Josh, Nick. I know this is no picnic for you."

"He's a great kid, Chloe. I can't thank you enough for giving me some time to get to know him." He put the dishes in the sink and folded his arms as he leaned back against the counter. "Look, I'm not going to pressure you. I know your mother is taking care of Josh tonight. But if you don't want to get together later, I understand."

"Oh, I want to." She turned to look up at him. "No question."

Heat flared in her eyes and he took her in his arms, pressing her against the sink as he kissed her. Lifting his head a fraction, he let out a breath. "I've wanted to do that all night."

She stroked his arm and rested her head on his shoulder the way he liked. "Mmm hmm. Me, too."

"Chloe, dear, bring in dessert?" Chloe's aunt said from the dining room.

Nick didn't want to let her go. Not yet. She felt so good up against him, finally losing some of that rigidity he'd sensed in her all evening. He nuzzled the silky skin on her nape, and she let out a sexy sigh. "Nick."

"The lemon bars, cuz!" Bo called, laughter in his voice.

Nick raised his head and took in a breath. "Lemon bars."

She kissed him lightly and gestured toward a plate on the counter, piled high with square yellow cakes covered with white icing. "Lemon bars." Picking one up, she held it to his lips. He bit into it, finding the pastry moist, sweet and tart.

"Mmm." He took her hand and brought the bar to her mouth. She took a bite and as she chewed he licked a bit if icing from the corner of her mouth. They were soon lost in another kiss. He could taste the lemon and sugar, and the hot sweetness that was purely Chloe.

Nick heard someone clear their throat and glanced over to find Laurel standing in the doorway. He ducked his head as Chloe squeezed past him to grab the plate of lemon bars.

"Don't mind me," Laurel chuckled.

She left the kitchen and Nick placed a hand on Chloe's arm to still her. "Come to the inn later?"

She stared up at him for a beat. "Yes."

He saw she still had a speck of icing on the corner of her bottom lip and he wanted to take her mouth again. "Bring a couple of those lemon bars," he said as she stepped past him.

Her lips parted as she grasped his meaning. She left the kitchen and Nick took a breath. What was he thinking, kissing her in her aunt's kitchen while a roomful of Butlers—including their son—sat close by? He ran his tongue over his lips. Man, she tasted better than those lemon bars, though.

He brushed a hand through his hair and returned to the dining room. "Well, I think I'll say good night."

"Won't you stay for dessert?" Chloe's mother asked.

He caught Chloe's gaze as her blue-gray eyes went wide. Oh, he wanted dessert. But later, with her. "No, thank you. But everything was delicious."

"Don't forget about Clone Wars tomorrow, Nick," Josh said, reaching for a lemon bar.

"No way," Nick smiled.

He said his goodnights and went out to the truck. Tonight had been surreal. Eating with Chloe's entire family, feeling like a part of something bigger than himself. Everyone had been so welcoming. Even Jack seemed to accept Nick's presence at the table. But for Chloe to give him the chance to get to know Josh, even a little bit? That was nearly as sweet as that last kiss he'd shared with her in the kitchen.

He went back to the inn to wait for her, working a little on his project notes to pass the time. He could only imagine what she'd gone through after his escape. He'd never met a group of people sharper than the Butlers. At least they wouldn't give her too hard of a time with Josh there.

Josh. The kid was pretty amazing. What would he be like if Nick had had a hand in raising him for the past five years? Yeah, he felt cheated. But even though he barely knew the Butlers, he'd bet he couldn't pick a better bunch of people to take care of his son. He deserved a chance to take care of him too, though. Now that the secret was out and he knew about him.

About an hour later, her knock came to his door. Just three soft raps and his blood started to pound. Chloe's knock. He pulled the door open, reaching out to grab Chloe to him before she could even say "hello."

"Baby, I've missed you," he said.

He kissed her and she wrapped one arm around his neck before leaning away from him. "Nick, wait."

"What?" He pulled back to find her holding up a little foil-wrapped plate and arched a brow. "Is that what I think it is?"

She grinned, the expression surprisingly hot.

"Lemon bars."

He growled low in his throat and pulled her closer. He soon had her naked on the big bed, wearing nothing but that expression he'd come to know. Desire was stamped on her beautiful face, her eyes dark and her lips parted. Taking one lemon bar from the plate, he made good use of its thick sweet icing. With his index finger he picked up a big dollop and traced it over her neck, her breasts, her belly. He kissed her again before licking it off of her.

"You taste so damn good, Chloe," he rasped.

She sighed and purred as he slowly licked the icing from her body. By the time it was gone he could hardly wait to finish what they'd started. But she made him wait, stroking his shoulders, his arms, until he was sticky with the stuff too. She used her lips and tongue on his body too, until both of them were breathing fast.

Finally, after he thought he would die before he could get inside of her, he was there. He took long slow strokes that brought him as close to her as he could get. She breathed his name and held on to him tight.

The air smelled like sugar and lemons and Chloe and he closed his eyes as she shattered beneath him. His climax struck in the next moment and he felt like it lasted forever.

She cuddled close to him, as was now her usual behavior, and he wrapped himself around her as they both came down. "Mmm, so sweet."

Giggling, Chloe flicked her tongue on the tip of his nose. "I don't think I'll ever look at a lemon bar the same way again."

He could feel the bits of icy hardening on his skin and saw she had a slight sheen on parts of her delectable body. He brought his face close to hers. "Looks like we'll have to take a bath," he said, feigning annoyance.

Chloe just smiled.

***

Nick stood on the porch of Chloe's house at five o'clock the next night, with two big bags of Chinese takeout held in his hands. When he'd seen her at the café this morning, she hadn't mentioned dinner but he didn't want to give her a chance to shorten tonight's visit. She would probably invite him to stay, since he'd been cool with Josh on two occasions now. But she seemed to have her own internal argument going on and he didn't want to give the "against" side any extra points. Besides, why should she wait on him? Didn't she wait on people all day, every day?

He knocked again and the door slowly opened, revealing his son hanging off the doorknob with a big smile on his face. Nick felt the porch rock beneath his feet but managed to smile back as he tried to catch his breath. "Hi, Josh."

"Hi, Nick." He released the knob and ran toward the back of the house. "Mommy, Nick's here!"

Nick stepped inside as Chloe emerged from what he guessed was the kitchen. "Hey."

Chloe smiled and stepped over to him. "What's this?"

Nick held up the bags. "Chinese. I didn't know what you or Josh liked so I got pretty much everything."

She laughed softly. "Thanks." She took one of the bags and turned. "Come on back."

Josh was sitting at a picnic table on the back deck with a pile of Legos spilled on the surface in front of him. Nick saw the deck wasn't much larger than the table itself.

Chloe put down the bag she held. "Nick brought

dinner, Josh."

The little boy looked up in question. "Yeah?"

"Chinese." Nick placed his bag on the table as Chloe pushed some stray Legos out of the way.

"I'll go get the plates," she said, heading back into the house.

"What do you like, Josh?" Nick asked. "I brought sweet-and-sour chicken, sauce on the side."

"The little chicken nuggets?"

"Yep." Nick sat across from Josh. "I didn't like the sauce when I was your age. I used to eat them with ketchup."

Josh blinked up at him. "That's how I eat 'em."

Nick managed to nod at that disclosure.

Chloe came back out onto the deck with a stack of dishes and napkins. "Can you grab the silverware?"

Nick stood and went into the kitchen. She'd told him that her brother had helped with the house when she'd first moved in and Nick spotted Jack's handiwork in here, seeing improvements that he guessed weren't original yet seemed to fit. The kitchen was still small, though. At least the window above the sink overlooked the deck and compact backyard. It was little wonder that Josh loved running around at Jack's place, although that big shaggy dog probably had something to do with that.

He grabbed the silverware and peeked out onto the deck. "Ketchup?"

"Refrigerator door," she answered.

He brought it out and they ate together, like the family they almost were. The family he couldn't help dreaming about. Josh told him all the plot points of the movie they were going to watch and Nick tried to keep things straight. The kid was smart for five, not that Nick had much exposure to kids of any age. Maybe he might be biased where his son was concerned, but he didn't care. Josh was amazing.

After dinner Nick was on the comfy couch with his son, sitting close together as the show played. Chloe came out and checked on them after tidying the kitchen, but she pretty much left them alone after she went down the hall to the bedrooms. He had to believe that she was softening toward his relationship with Josh. He so wanted to believe that this was building toward some sort of relationship.

The boy seemed to warm to him, snuggling close as

the bad guys tried to capture the rebel heroes. To Nick this felt like the most natural thing in the world, sitting there with his arm draped over his son's little shoulders as they talked about one character or another. He might have missed a lot with Josh, but if Chloe let him he would give his right arm for the chance to make up for lost time.

Chloe came back into the living room some time later, obviously after showering. Her hair was in damp waves and she smelled so sweet he could hardly concentrate. She made some popcorn for them to share but didn't join them on the couch. She curled up on the only other piece of furniture in the room, a fat chair wrapped in a thick cotton slipcover like the couch. She held a book in her hands, a smile on her lips as she apparently caught snatches of his and Josh's conversation.

Nick looked around the house as they sat there. Chloe and Josh both needed more space. Josh needed a big playroom, and a bigger backyard for that matter. An idea for the perfect home for his family began to form in his mind. Big kitchen, lots of storage. A playroom off of the kitchen so they could keep an eye on Josh while they cooked together. A huge owners' suite and bath… He ruthlessly set all of those tempting thoughts aside. He knew he was lucky that Chloe was letting him spend time with Josh at this point. But should he dare to dream they could be a family? He wasn't that big a fool. She had yet to accept his apology for his screw-up in Reno, and it was still hanging unspoken between them.

It was nearly eight o'clock by the time the end credits rolled, and Josh yawned loudly. The popcorn was long gone and it was probably getting to be time for Nick to make his exit.

"Okay, honey," Chloe said. "Why don't you go brush your teeth and put on your pjs."

Josh sighed but trudged away. He could hear the little boy washing and getting ready for bed in the bathroom about halfway down the hall. He caught bits of Josh's voice humming the music from the movie and Nick smiled to himself.

He looked over at Chloe. "Thanks. Tonight was pretty amazing."

"You're good with him, Nick." She almost sounded surprised.

He felt a flicker of irritation. "I told you that I

would never hurt him," he said, his voice low. "And if you would only accept my apology, you would know that I would never hurt you again."

"Don't." She shook her head. "Tonight was one night. And this has nothing to do with you and me."

He scoffed. "I think this has something to do with you and me."

She opened her mouth, and he could just imagine some of the things she wanted to say. But at that moment Josh came back in, looking so cute in his Star Wars pajamas that Nick put aside any animosity toward Chloe and her trademark stubbornness.

"Can I say good night to Nick?"

Chloe's lips thinned but she nodded. "Sure, honey."

Josh jumped on the couch and wrapped his arms around Nick's neck. Nick didn't know what to do for a second, and then he hugged him back. This was something else, holding his son for the first time. His eyes stung with tears and he held his breath until he forced himself to loosen his grip.

Josh squeezed him one more time then climbed down. "Tuck me in, Mommy."

"Be there in a minute, honey."

Josh ran back down the hall and Nick stood to face her.

"Thanks," he said again.

Chloe was all stiff and prickly again. *Damn it.*

"Good night, Chloe." He left her in the home she'd made for their son, without him or his help, and returned to the inn.

Chapter 17

By Friday afternoon Nick was mired in paperwork. He reviewed emails by the dozens, more than a few Fed exes from legal and design, as well as information from the county and state agencies. There was a lot to consider for the project, and there was no way he was going to let anything slip through the cracks. Phone calls from his dad proved to him that Joe was eager to help in any way. He seemed to be completely behind Nick, seeming to take his cue from Nick when he laid everything out as answers came back.

Nick hadn't been this excited about a project in years. As preliminary designs came back from Stockton, he began to fool around with the plans that had been niggling at the back of his mind since that night at Chloe's.

He wanted the house to reflect what he knew about her. From the decorations at the café and the way she dressed her little house, she obviously liked things simple and comfortable, yet aesthetically pleasing and functional. He knew that she wasn't a formal person, so having large open spaces that flowed from one room to another would make the most sense for the floor plan. He marveled that he knew so much about a woman he hadn't seen in years and only spent a handful of days with this time around. But it was as if he'd always known her. It was really too bad that she refused to get to know him.

He took a breath and returned to sketching. Josh needed a large playroom, so that if he did leave clutter around Chloe wouldn't feel stressed trying to always keep it picked up and put away. Nick had been a boy once, and he knew that the older boys got the more toys they accumulated. And the larger the toys tended to get, too. Built-in cubbies and plenty of storage was needed too, in the playroom and in Josh's room.

After creating an owner's suite with an adjacent bathroom Chloe would revel in, he turned his attention to the back of the house. Chloe deserved a large efficient kitchen. A work island, a breakfast bar with plenty of seating for various Butlers who might stop by for dinner. His pencil moved quickly over the paper as he sketched in the details. He could almost picture Josh in the dining alcove he created near the bay window, dunking his cookies into a big glass of milk. Nick smiled. Of course, his son would be a dunker. Like his father before him.

Recalling how small the deck at Chloe's house was, he decided that they needed more room there in this plan. But maybe, like at Jack's cabin, the deck should be nearly bare of furnishings. Jack and Laurel didn't eat out there, so close to the wilderness. No one would eat out on this deck either. Nick stilled, his pencil poised above the drawing as the inevitable struck him. He wanted to put this imaginary house in the Big Bend community. Since there would be lots of nature around the individual yards, he didn't want any animals to come up on the deck. But a big backyard like Jack's? His son would love to have that. The kid deserved it. And when the surveyors finished the plot plans Nick would pick out the prime location for this particular house.

He took out his laptop and opened the design program. Transferring his renderings seemed to bring the place to life. Soon he could feel the flow of the space, and he added the details that were both pleasing and practical. A few more clicks and the rough sketch looked nearly as solid as the house would be someday.

He stared at the spaces on the screen in front of him. He could almost hear the laughter from the family room, the clinking of dishes in the kitchen. The splashes from the big bathtub in Josh's bathroom. A sudden bitterness rose in his throat.

He wouldn't picture himself in this house with Chloe and Josh. He couldn't. Not after their argument last night. She'd made it perfectly clear that his getting to know Josh at least superficially was okay but he wasn't to expect anything more from Chloe than what he was getting now. Sex with no real interaction aside from the occasional dinner.

Yeah, the sex was great. The best he'd ever had. Yeah, he felt that connection to her growing stronger every day. And although she seemed to like being around him, both in bed and out of it, she still kept him at arm's length emotionally.

That soured his mood. He saved the design and set aside plans for the house he would most likely never live in and instead considered those of strangers lucky enough to find a home there.

The houses the Stockton design team came up with were all on a large scale, and seemed to incorporate what he'd related to them. Any of the plans would appeal to the demographic they were trying to attract. Simple yet high-tech, comfortable yet accessible. Families would love these, as would empty-nesters who never seem to keep their nest quite as empty as they might like. Families like the Butlers. Warm and welcoming, if a little intrusive. It was clear that they had Chloe and Josh's best interests at heart, and he couldn't help but take satisfaction in guessing that at least a few of them seemed to think *he* just might be the best for them.

"Why won't you let me in, Chloe?" He set aside the renderings as well and turned off the desk lamp. "Even a little bit?"

***

Chloe sat in the living room again, the book in her lap forgotten. She couldn't get the image of Nick and their son out of her mind. The two of them talking so easily out on the deck and, later, sitting like buddies on the couch sharing a movie and a bowl of popcorn. It scared the heck out of her, and Nick's insistence that she put aside their past, that she forget his betrayal in Reno, caused her stomach to churn. How could he expect her to ever trust him again? With Josh, yes. He seemed trustworthy on that count, and she knew in her heart that he would never hurt their son. But could she trust him with her heart? She couldn't be half as sure about that.

Was she being stubborn? She shook her head. No. That morning was still as clear as crystal in her mind. How long would it be before he got tired of her and fell into bed with the closest available woman?

"I'm not going to put myself out there again," she murmured.

But she could admit to herself that the feel of Nick's arms around her, their easy conversations and incredible passion, was something she would give her eyeteeth to hold on to. And she couldn't ignore how much he was coming to love their son. She slammed the book shut. Growling softly, she stood and paced the living room. Her emotions were dragging her down again. Her control was slipping and she couldn't afford to lose it now. She went to Josh's toy bins and began to sort Lego blocks, first by color and then by size. It didn't matter that the minute Josh played with them again they would be in a jumble. For tonight, the simple act of organizing them soothed her.

About twenty minutes later she sat back and

observed her work. That satisfaction that came from bringing order to chaos seemed lesser tonight somehow. Though her pulse had slowed and her breathing had eased, her nerves were still frayed. Forcing her hands to unclench, she closed her eyes and breathed deeply. She recognized the unease for what it was now. She wanted Nick. Not just in bed, though that was amazing. No. She wanted him to stay with her and Josh. She wanted him to stay forever.

She took in a shuddering breath. At last she could admit it to herself as silent tears slipped beneath her lashes.

She wanted him to love her.

***

Nick hadn't heard from Chloe Friday night but that wasn't going to stop him from going to the café the next morning. Incredibly, Jack had called that afternoon and invited him to go fishing with him and Josh. He'd never been in his life, but he would be damned if he missed the opportunity to spend more time with his son. So here he was, up with the birds again, with his newly-purchased gear stowed in the Ridgeline.

When he walked into the café, his eyes immediately settled on Chloe where she stood at the service counter.

Like that first day weeks ago, he appreciated her body, and all that beautiful wavy hair. But she meant so much more to him now. He waved to Jack where he sat with Laurel at what he guessed was their usual table and stepped over to the counter.

"Chloe."

She turned, her eyes going round. "Nick. What are you doing here?"

He tamped down his irritation at her tone. "Jack invited me fishing." He let that sink in for a moment. "With him and Josh."

She glanced over at Jack, who met her gaze evenly. Nick didn't miss the smile on Laurel's face, though.

Chloe's eyes narrowed. "I guess that's okay."

"Jeez, I should hope so," he said.

She stepped closer, her expression contrite. "I'm sorry, Nick. I know you deserve this time with Josh. I appreciate your patience."

He wanted to shake her but affected a carefree stance. "It's just fishing, Chloe."

She studied his face for a moment and Nick bit his tongue. Let her think this was only fishing to him. If she believed that for a second, she really didn't know him at all.

"Hi, Nick!"

Josh came running out of the back like last Saturday, only this time he came right up to him. Nick relished the feel of Josh's small arms wrapped around his legs while he touched the boy's hair. "Hey, Josh."

Josh squeezed him and looked up at him. "You're coming with me and Uncle Jack?"

"Yep."

Josh's face grew serious as he stepped back. "You know you have to be quiet, right?"

"Yeah, I heard that."

"And you have to sit still for a long time?"

Nick hid his smile. "Yeah, I heard that too."

Josh nodded. "Good." He ran over to Jack. "Let's go, Uncle Jack. Nick knows the rules."

Nick looked over at Chloe as Jack stood and said good bye to Laurel. Yeah, he knew the rules. But Chloe better watch out. He planned to change them and soon.

On the ride through the Forest in Jack's Cherokee, Josh kept a steady stream of chatter. He wore Jack's

Ranger hat, and couldn't have looked more adorable. Nick refrained from taking his picture with his phone. What would the kid think? Nick wouldn't need a picture, though. He would never forget that little face beaming from underneath that wide brim.

"This is the spot Josh and I usually go to," Jack said. "There's an outcropping and a good place to stand or sit on the bank."

"So we don't wade into the water?"

"No." Jack glanced over at him. "You didn't bring waders, did you?"

Nick laughed. "After you called me I went to the outfitters and bought just about everything."

Jack smiled. "Maybe sometime just you and I can go."

Nick's brows rose. Now that was a stamp of approval if he'd ever heard one.

Jack turned off into an area of the Forest that Nick hadn't explored yet and pulled the Cherokee to a stop. They gathered their packs and rods. Nick helped Josh down from the backseat and the little boy grabbed his pack and hurried toward Jack. Nick grabbed his pack, leaving the duffle stuffed with waders he wouldn't need, and soon the three of them were trudging through the woods down toward a graceful bend in the river.

Nick saw that Josh grabbed hold of Jack's back belt loop as they hiked, yet another sign of the routine and familiar. He ignored the pang that settled around his heart. Josh was lucky to have Jack in his life. Nick just had to get used to it and not let it tear him up inside.

"Uncle Jack has the coolest bugs, Nick."

"Flies, Josh," Jack corrected. They settled down and Jack opened his tackle box. Nick looked at the array of fuzzy lures. He'd never been fly-fishing himself, but they sure did look pretty cool.

"They don't really look like flies," Josh said. "But they fool the fish."

Nick nodded sagely. "I bet."

Josh held his hands behind his back and nodded his little chin toward the tackle box. "The purple, Uncle Jack."

"Josh knows not to touch the lures, since they have hooks." Jack took up the selected fly and tied it to the line on Josh's short rod. The little boy settled on the bank and let Jack cast his line for him. "Josh is using an attractor. It doesn't have to look exactly like the bug it's supposed to be."

Jack held up another lure, and Nick noticed that this one looking a lot like a real bug. "This is an imitator. It's supposed to look like a mayfly." Nick watched him take care of his own line and followed suit with the lure Jack chose for him.

Standing with Jack, his son between them, seemed surreal. Jack was a quiet guy, so Nick was spared the task of making small talk. Josh kept up a steady stream of chatter, though.

"The fish like it real quiet, Nick."

"Uh huh," Nick answered softly.

"Uncle Jack says that if we talk too much we won't catch anything."

Nick caught Jack's eye and found him smiling. Why did he think that they didn't usually catch anything?

"Uncle Jack's a Forest Ranger."

"I know. Pretty cool, huh?"

"Uh huh." Josh's line bobbed as he gestured up toward the trees. "But Bo is a tracker."

"A tracker?" Nick asked.

Jack nodded. "Bo is the best tracker in Yuma County."

"So the Butlers know the Forest pretty well."

"I thought Chloe brought you hiking."

"She did. On our hike last week she showed me some great spots I never would have discovered on my own."

"Yeah, the Butlers know the Forest. Any one of us would be a great guide." Jack took up his line and cast it again. "How's your project coming?"

"Very well, thanks. I think once it goes public, the interest will be pretty high."

Jack gazed across the river. "You'd be hard-pressed to find a prettier place to live."

"I could live here forever," Nick admitted.

Jack cocked a brow. "Forever? That's a long time. Way longer than a few weeks."

Nick knew what he was getting at. "I think I'm ready for forever, Jack."

Jack fell quiet again, as did Nick. Let Jack make of it what he would. Nick wanted to stay in Cloud Canyon with Chloe and their son. It was as clear as the water lapping against the bank.

After a bit, they set down their rods and shared the protein bars Jack had brought along. Nick brought some snacks, too. Gummy worms for Josh and spicy chips for him and Jack. After eating and tucking all their trash back into their packs, Jack showed Nick how to tie a fly. It was an amazing process, and Josh watched wide-eyed as Nick created a bug out of blue thread and feathers. He used a dry-fly hook on his, like the one Jack had given him that floated on top of the water. The fly was a little lopsided but the expression on Josh's face made Nick feel pretty proud of it.

"Wow," Josh said around a mouthful of gummies. "Uncle Jack's gonna show me how to do that someday. Right now I just get to watch him make bugs."

"Use a wet-fly hook on the next one, Nick," Jack said, handing him a thicker, heavier hook. "I'll show you how to make a nymph imitator that sinks below the surface."

"Why would you want it to sink?" Nick asked.

Jack met his gaze. "Sometimes you can only catch what you want if you dive a little bit deeper."

Nick blinked as he worked the guy's words in his head. Suddenly, he grasped his meaning and nodded. He had to go all in if he wanted a life with Chloe and their son. Only the stakes were much higher here than he'd ever encountered in Reno.

He finished tying the fly and held it up for their inspection. "A nymph imitator. Sort of."

"You're gettin' good at that, Nick," Josh said.

"Not too shabby," Jack added. "Maybe the next time we come we'll use Nick's flies."

Nick threw him a grateful look, at which Jack nodded. If he had his way he would be here with Josh, fishing and hiking and making a life, forever.

Chapter 18

Chloe picked up her cell on the first ring. Reading the display, she hesitated to answer. *Nick.* Things had been strained between them since the night he was here, and she really didn't know where they stood. She could hardly believe her brother invited him to go fishing with Josh. That just blew her mind. And Nick had gone with them. Wow.

Would Nick want to stay around Cloud Canyon? The attractions were tame compared to Reno. The Nick she knew there had been out for kicks, high stakes and strong drinks. But the Nick she was getting to know here? Considerate lover, attentive father, focused businessman? She believed she might like this Nick a whole lot better.

Taking a breath, she pressed the button and answered. "Hey, Nick."

"Chloe."

Her name, said in that sexy voice, sent her pulse racing. She was truly pitiful.

"What's up?" she asked.

"I wondered if you wanted to grab dinner?"

She ran one hand over the slipcover on the big

chair, smoothing out a few wrinkles. "Dinner?"

"Yeah. I know Josh will be at Jack and Laurel's tonight."

"How do you—? Oh, yeah. You were with Jack earlier."

"And Josh," he added, a challenge in his voice.

"How, um… How did that go?"

He laughed softly, which soothed the tension in her muscles as her breathing eased. "We didn't catch anything."

She smiled. "Jack and Josh hardly ever catch anything."

"Our son is a chatterbox. That's no big surprise. I was too, when I was his age."

She bit her lip. It was so tempting to learn more about the father of her child, what he was like growing up, what made him into the man he'd become. She couldn't afford to give in to that temptation, though. Not if she wanted to keep her heart out of it all.

"I don't know about dinner, Nick."

She heard him expel a breath. "Listen, we don't have to do anything fancy. What about The Antler?"

"Seriously?"

"Yeah. If you want, you can even meet me there."

He was giving her both control and freedom. Control over if they would get together or not and the freedom to leave when she chose to. The only trouble was she didn't know what to do with all that power.

"Okay." She glanced at the clock on the side table. It was a little after seven. "What time?"

"How about eight?"

"Sure."

"Great." She imagined she could see his heart-stopping smile. "See you then."

They disconnected and she stood there for a moment. Meeting Nick at The Antler. It seemed so normal. What any couple might do.

She went into her bedroom and pulled on one of Laurel's tops, this one in shades of pink. Her jeans would be fine for dinner at the bar, so she just slid on a pair of sandals, pulled her hair back with a headband and put on a little make-up. Stalling for time, she grabbed a thin cardigan and stared hard at her reflection in the bathroom mirror. She let out a soft curse. "When did this get so difficult?"

Not dating, really. She hadn't really dated in her life so she had no point of reference. No, being with Nick was what was getting more difficult every time. It was hard to distance herself and hard to deny that she was in love with him again. "Fool, fool, fool."

She turned out the light and left the house, bound for The Antler. When she pulled into the parking lot, she wasn't surprised to find it nearly full. There wasn't a lot to do in Cloud Canyon on a Saturday night, not that she'd ever been one for the bar scene. Heck, she hadn't even been old enough to drink when she met Nick and got pregnant with Josh.

As she pulled open the front door, the sounds of the bar hit her first. Music and chatter, and the occasion crack of a ball at the pool table to the right. She hadn't been in the place in ages, but it hadn't really changed much. Running her gaze over the bar against the back wall, she saw it was two people deep.

"Chloe!"

She turned and found Nick standing several feet to her left, his hand raised. She waved and started to walked over to him. A woman, apparently an out-of-towner, bumped into him as she drew near, obviously a deliberate move, and smiled up at him. "'Scuse me, honey." She ran a hand over his arm. "Are you visiting, too?"

Nick smiled at her as he eased her hand from him, but Chloe felt the impact of the expression. Apparently so did the woman. She looked like she wanted to rub herself against him.

Nick untangled himself and reached for Chloe. "About time you got here."

He kissed her, tender and sweet, and there was no denying the message that sent to the other woman. Chloe returned the kiss and when he lifted his head she absently noticed the woman was gone.

"You look great."

"Thanks."

"You want a drink?"

She nodded and looked around the bar. She noticed that more than one woman looked at Nick with obvious hunger as they stood there. Yes, the man looked good. He wore jeans and a soft cotton Henley that made her want to rip off its buttons. He was tall and strong and so beautiful.

She touched his arm, letting a little bit of possessiveness show. "I'd love a beer."

His eyes sparkled as he stroked her hand resting on his arm. "Yeah, me too." A booth nearby cleared out and he ushered her onto the seat. "Let me go tell the bartender to send a waitress over."

Chloe watched him go, admiring his butt. Mmm. She placed her sweater on the seat and played with the strap of her little purse as she looked around the place. She recognized a few faces from the café and around town, but the bar was filled with mostly out-of-towners. Nick returned with two open bottles of beer and she took a long swig of hers. Another woman walked by their table, slow and deliberate as she looked Nick up and down before finally making her way past them. Chloe drank more of her beer.

"You better go easy," Nick laughed. "We haven't eaten yet."

He waved a hand and a waitress came over and took their order. Barbeque sandwiches, pork for him and chicken for her, and fries. Bar food. She rarely ate bar food.

After the waitress left, Nick fingered his bottle of

beer as he stared at the tabletop. "Today was amazing, Chloe. And not just being with Josh and your brother. The Forest is incredible." He raised his eyes to meet hers and she was captivated by the intensity in their crystal blue depths. "I could stay here forever."

Her heart began to pound. Forever? She drained her beer before answering. "Nick—"

"Hey, cuz!"

Chloe turned as Bo and Krissy came up to their table. "Hi, Bo." She met Krissy's gaze and managed to nod. "Krissy."

Krissy fidgeted beside Bo, her brow knit, before finally turning toward Nick. To Chloe's surprise the expression on her face was one she hadn't expected. It was open, honest and friendly, without an ounce of flirtation. Weird.

"Nick, I heard back from your father," Krissy said. "Stockton won the bid and will work on the Lake Tahoe project."

"Krissy's going to be their sales contact," Bo added.

"Lake Tahoe?" Chloe asked.

Nick nodded. "I know my father was all for it." He

took a swig of his beer. "He wanted me to head this one."

"But what about Big Bend?" Chloe asked before she could stop herself.

Nick met her gaze, unwavering as he set his bottle down. "I told him I'm committed to this project. I'm not going to work on Lake Tahoe."

Chloe blinked. Wasn't this what she wanted? Nick's commitment? She found Bo eyeing her closely and Krissy cleared her throat.

"This is a huge project, Nick," Krissy said. "It could be worth millions. Your father told me he thought you'd jump at the chance."

Nick shook his head. "My father doesn't know what's at stake here."

Bo looked between Nick and Chloe, apparently seeing something she'd hoped to keep hidden. Oh, was she that transparent? That desperate? Did every emotion show on her face now?

Bo nodded to both of them, taking Krissy's elbow as the waitress brought their food to the table. "Come on, Krissy. Let them eat." He met Chloe's gaze dead on, approval clear in his Butler blue eyes. "See you later, cuz."

She huffed out a breath. Darn Bo, anyway. He never missed a thing. "Later."

She nodded and asked the waitress for another beer. She hardly touched her food as they sat there. The bar felt close and stifling as the truth of Nick's words struck her. He was staying here. He was turning down the opportunity for an obviously lucrative project. He'd told her that he wanted to make his father sit up and take notice for once. Wasn't a multimillion-dollar project the best way to do that?

Instead, he wanted to stay here in Cloud Canyon. He'd actually said those words. She could barely breathe. Their conversation was all but one-sided, with Nick talking about the Forest, about Josh, about the Big Bend project. She nodded or mumbled something in response now and then, unable to get her mind past the fact that he planned to stay here. How would she be able to hide her feelings for him if he stayed here?

Over an hour later, Nick's plate was empty. She'd had four beers and maybe that many fries.

"You didn't eat much. Did you want something else?"

She considered his question, her mind fuzzy. "What?"

His brow furrowed for a moment. "Why don't I take you home?"

She managed a nod. Nick stood and she placed her hands on the table, her legs shaking as she pushed herself up to stand.

"Whoa," he said, grabbing her around the waist. "I shouldn't have let you order that last beer."

"I don't drink much," she murmured.

"Yeah, I get that." He signaled to Bo, who came over. "I'm taking her home. Can you take care of her car?"

"Sure." Bo looked at Chloe but she could barely make out his features. Was he smiling? "'Night, cuz."

She closed her eyes and the place tilted beneath her. Whoa. Big mistake. Leaning heavily on Nick, she let him all but pull her out of the bar and help her into his truck.

***

Nick watched Chloe out of the corner of his eye as he drove to her little house. He pulled up in front and stopped, setting the brake. He reached over and touched her shoulder. "You okay?"

"Mmm."

Man, she was pretty wasted. She did look sweet, though. All curled up toward him, her expression soft.

He brought his face close to hers. "Keys, Chloe."

Chloe opened one eye and smiled sleepily up at him. "Keys, Nick," she sighed.

He blew out a breath. "No, baby. I need your keys to get into the house."

"Oh." She cuddled into the seat. "Mmm, comfy." She shut her eyes again. "My purse."

Nick shuffled through the items in her bag, finally jangling the keys in his hand. "I'll come around and get you."

His got out and went around to her side. Easing the door open, he caught her in his arms. He shut the door and shifted to put her on her feet. He urged her along the walk to the front door and let them into her house. "We're almost there."

"Almost there," she softly repeated.

"Your bedroom's back here?" he asked, leading her down the hallway.

She nodded, obviously trying to rouse herself as she

blinked rapidly. "Jeez, I only had three—no, four—beers."

"And no food," he added.

She laughed softly. "That was the clincher."

He got her onto her bed and eased off her shoes and most of her clothes. She settled back into the pillows and closed her eyes.

"Bo said he'll get your car in the morning." He dropped a kiss on her lips. "Good night."

She wrapped her arms around him and pulled him closer. "Kiss me again, Nick."

"Baby, you're not in any shape to invite me into your bed."

"But I want you."

She opened her eyes, and he thought he could get lost in their depths. Though a little out of focus, her gaze was soft and tender. "Chloe."

Her bottom lip poked out a little. "Don't you want me anymore?"

He smiled at the ridiculous question. "I'll always want you."

"So many other women, Nick," she murmured. "So many want you."

He took her hands from around his neck and kissed each one. "I don't know who you're talking about but I don't want anyone else."

Her eyes rounded for a moment. "Really?" When he nodded she let her eyes close in apparent relief. "I love you, Nick."

He straightened and stood beside Chloe's bed, stunned. She loved him. She'd said that once, in Reno. He'd said it back, for the first and last time in his memory, and he'd known for a while now that he still loved her. Grabbing a quilt from an antique rack near her bed, he covered her and kissed her cheek. Yeah, she smelled like beer but he also caught that Chloe-scent of flowers and cinnamon.

He brushed aside a lock of her hair, letting his fingers trace over her temple. She sighed and turned into his hand. Man, she would have a hell of a headache in the morning. He went into the small bathroom off her bedroom and grabbed a bottle of aspirin from the medicine cabinet. After filling a glass with water, he left both on her nightstand.

"Good night, Chloe." He kissed her again, softly. "I

love you, too."

He left her purse and keys in the kitchen, locked up the house and started back to the inn. What had happened tonight to upset her enough to drink like that? Yeah, there was that woman who came on to him hard at the bar, but he hadn't spared her any notice. Then Krissy and Bo had stopped at their table. His hands fisted on the wheel for a moment. *Krissy.*

That was when Chloe had started drinking and stopped eating. But Krissy hadn't been flirting, and she hadn't acted anything less than all business. Hell, even Bo had been there. If it wasn't Krissy or that other woman, then what happened to set Chloe off?

Her sweet words before he left echoed in his ears. She loved him. She'd actually said she loved him.

"She better remember this tomorrow," he said.

Chapter 19

Chloe rolled over and reached across the bed for
Nick. There was nothing but quilt in her grasp and she
squinted one eye open. Faded flowers on a cream
background. Not the buffalo plaid at the Treetop. What...?
Oh! She was in her own bed. That explained why she was
alone. Nick wouldn't be here with her. Not in her house.
Then why did she have the feeling that he was here last
night?

She rolled onto her back, wincing as her stomach
rebelled. Hungry and nauseated at the same time, she tried
to move her tongue in her mouth and found it fat and fuzzy.
What the heck happened? It hit her all at once then. The
Antler. Nick and so many women undressing his beautiful
body with their eyes. Her drinking too many beers and him
helping her into bed. And then... something. A sweet kiss,
a tender stroke of his fingers, and— She sat up, crying out
softly as her head began to pound. Oh God, she'd told Nick
she loved him!

Grabbing the quilt in both fists, she took shallow
breaths until the pounding in her head eased a bit. She saw
the bottle of aspirin and a glass of water on her nightstand

and knew that was Nick's handiwork. Well, at least he hadn't run screaming from the room after her ridiculous confession. She swallowed two aspirin and drained the water in a few gulps, settling back against the headboard and closing her eyes. She'd told Nick she loved him.

"Chloe, you are such a fool."

Tears squeezed from her aching eyelids as she indulged herself in a moment of regret for the ultimate insanity. Not only had she fallen for Nick again, she'd told him so. She set the glass back on the nightstand and took a mental inventory of herself. She was only wearing her bra and panties, which meant he'd taken off her clothes. There was little she remembered past the second beer at The Antler, aside from Nick's conversation about Big Bend and his decision to stay in Cloud Canyon.

"Fat chance he'll stay now," she whispered.

She focused on the clock beside her and saw it was nearly ten. Thank goodness Josh was at Jack and Laurel's. She could barely take care of herself right now, let alone her little boy. Just imagining his steady stream of chatter caused her teeth to ache.

Gingerly, she got up and made her way into the

bathroom. After a long shower, she felt more like herself. More aspirin and some of Josh's honey-nut cereal rings and soon she was nearly back to normal. Her phone dinged and she saw she had a text message waiting. It was from Bo. She read it, learning that he'd brought her Wrangler back to the house for her. She clicked her tongue. Only Bo could manage to smirk in a text. He'd been with Krissy, just like Nick had said last week. That was weird. And amazingly, Krissy was about the only woman in the place who hadn't looked like she was dying to catch Nick and mount him on their wall like the animal trophies in the bar.

There was no message from Nick. No real surprise there. He was probably packing up his stuff right now. At least Josh had no idea who he really was. You can't miss someone you never really knew, can you?

She thought about how much she'd missed Nick after Reno. "Yeah, you can."

Fresh tears burned her eyes and she dashed a hand over her cheeks. "Enough, Chloe Butler. You did fine without Nick six years ago. You'll do fine without him now."

She sat on the couch and cuddled a pillow to her

chest. "Keep telling yourself that," she sobbed.

***

By the time he'd gotten up, showered and dressed Nick realized he had nowhere to go. The café was closed and he couldn't expect a call from Chloe this morning. She was probably fighting one hell of a hangover anyway. He glanced at his phone and found a message from Jack waiting. He dialed his voicemail and learned that he and Laurel wanted him to come over again for dinner. Josh would be there. And maybe Chloe. He had to talk to her, get her to admit sober what she'd said drunk. She loved him. Well, he loved her and was staying in Cloud Canyon. They had to finally face what happened in Reno and hopefully she would accept his apology. Then maybe they could both move forward together.

He called Jack and accepted his invitation, then made a couple cups of coffee in his room and ate from the snack bar. Opening his laptop, he read through some emails from Joe and reviewed the designs. Once more his father pushed for him to jump on board the Lake Tahoe project, but Nick sent back his answer in the negative again.

Around five o'clock he started to pack up his work

to get ready for dinner at Jack and Laurel's.

He didn't see Chloe's Wrangler in front of Jack's cabin when he pulled up, but maybe she was coming later. God knew she would need some time today. He knew he should feel bad about her overindulgence last night, but it had broken down those damn walls of hers and let her finally truly admit their connection. He had to tread carefully, but he'd make her see that they belonged together. The two of them and Josh.

Laurel opened the door as he stepped up on the porch. "Hi, Nick. Josh said he saw your truck."

"Hi, Nick!" Josh came running toward him and hugged Nick's legs like before. "We've been waiting for you."

"Well, for Nick and your Mommy," Laurel said.

"Where is Mommy?"

Nick shrugged and looked at Laurel. Jack came in then, glancing around Nick as he obviously thought he'd be bringing Chloe with him. "Where's Chloe?"

"I guess she's a little late," Laurel said. She turned Josh toward a hallway off the great room. "Go wash up, honey. We'll eat when Mommy gets here."

Jack stepped over to Nick and handed him a beer. "Heard you and Chloe were at The Antler last night."

Nick arched a brow. "Bo?"

"Yep. He's got a mouth on him."

"Yeah." Nick lowered his voice. "Chloe had a little too much to drink."

Jack chuckled. "Bo told me that, too. Chloe doesn't usually drink."

"I got that." Nick walked over to the tall granite counter and leaned an elbow on it. "Something happened to set her off. I have no idea what, though."

"Really?" Jack took a pull on his beer, his brow furrowed. "Bo said she didn't look upset."

"Not upset, really. But something was bothering her."

Jack clapped him on the shoulder. "Well, thanks for getting her home safe."

"Of course."

Laurel and Josh returned just as a knock came at the door. Laurel went to answer as Josh ran up to Nick.

"Nick, I have to show you this new guy," Josh said, holding up an action figure. "Grandma got it for me."

Nick took the toy in his hand, a guy with armor sort of like he'd seen in the kid's show. "Was this guy in the movie we watched?"

"Nope. But he's in the second one. Come over and watch it with me."

"I'd love to, buddy. We'll have to check with your mom first, though."

"Check with me about what?" Chloe asked.

Nick turned to find her walking toward them. She looked a little pale, and maybe there were shadows beneath her eyes, but what really troubled him was the expression on her face. It was set, her gaze holding none of the softness he'd seen last night.

"Hey. Josh was just asking me over to watch another movie."

Something flickered across her face, gone in an instant. It almost looked like pain. "Sure. Nick can come over to watch with you, Josh."

Brr. Her tone was almost as chilly as when he'd first rolled into Cloud Canyon weeks ago. Laurel looked from one to the other, then gently took Josh's shoulder. "Let's go see if Uncle Jack needs any help, Josh."

Laurel took an oblivious Josh out onto the deck and Chloe stepped over to shut the door.

She seemed to take a breath then turned to face him. "Nick, we have to talk."

"If this is about last night—"

"It's not about last night. Well, not entirely. We need to set some ground rules if you plan to stick around."

"If?" Nick stepped closer. "Chloe, what's up with you? I told you last night that I plan to stay in Cloud Canyon."

She shook her head, her eyes downcast. "You shouldn't."

"Why the hell not?"

She faced him then, steely determination in those blue-gray eyes. "This is over."

His heart dropped to the bottom of his stomach. "No." He reached for her but she flinched. Fisting his hand, he let it drop it to his side. "Why?"

"Look, this wasn't what we agreed to. It's become… too much."

"For me? No, it isn't too much for me." She looked away and anger flared within him. And the certainty that she was trying her best to end what had really only just begun. "Maybe it's too much for you."

She spun toward him. "What?"

"You won't let me in, Chloe. It's as plain and simple as that."

Tears swam in her eyes but he had to press on. He had to let her know what she was doing to him. To them.

"I want to stay here with you. With Josh. Why can't you understand that?"

"You can still see Josh. I would never keep him from you again."

He snorted. "That's something, at least. But there's nothing between us, huh?"

"No." She brushed her hair back, frowning as it tugged her probably still tender scalp. "Nothing."

He took her arm and pulled her close. "You told me you love me, Chloe. Last night, you told me you love me."

"I was drunk."

He dropped her arm. "I wasn't."

"What?"

"I was stone sober when I told you I loved you, too."

She just stared at him.

"Why can't you admit your feelings today, huh?" he asked. "What are you afraid of?"

Josh opened the door and Laurel followed close behind. "Wait, honey."

"Why can't you admit it?" Nick went on.

"Look, go take the big job in Lake Tahoe." She waved a hand in the air. "Make a name for yourself, like you always wanted. We're finished."

He heard Laurel gasp but he tried to keep it together. Josh stood there, his eyes round, as he watched his mother start to cry. That was it. He wouldn't drag their son into this mess. And he wouldn't be made into the bad guy, either.

"I'm through, Chloe." He walked toward the front door. "Through trying to prove myself to you. Through trying to apologize for something that happened years ago. And through trying to get just a little bit of affection out of you."

"Nick," Laurel said, but Nick held up one hand.

"Thanks for the invitation, Laurel. But I'll have to take a rain check on dinner."

He left before he said anything more. Damn right he would still get to see Josh. Maybe he needed to talk to lawyer and assert his rights in case Chloe changed her mind.

He got into the truck and slammed the door, his eyes pricking with tears. He slammed a hand on the steering wheel and felt a tear leak out from beneath his lashes. "Damn you, Chloe."

And just like that, he'd lost everything he'd only just realized he'd always wanted.

***

"What the hell is wrong with you?" Jack asked.

Chloe turned to face her brother. "Please, Jack—

"Don't, Chloe." He glanced at Laurel and Josh, and she followed his gaze. Josh looked about ready to cry.

"Why did Nick leave, Mommy?"

"He had to, honey," she managed to say.

Her stomach churned from the tears longing to escape, and her throat ached with the sobs she kept locked inside so she wouldn't completely freak him out. "Nick wasn't going to stay in Cloud Canyon."

Josh shook his head. "That's not what he told me

and Uncle Jack."

Jack placed a hand on Josh's shoulder. "Come on, Josh. I bet Smokey would like to have a catch."

Josh stared at Chloe and then at the front door, a flare of hope on his little face. "Nick's really gone?"

Jack ushered him back outside without answering, but she hadn't missed the disapproval on her brother's face. She sank down onto the leather couch and buried her face in her hands. "God, what a mess."

"You made this one yourself."

She glanced up at Laurel. "It was only a matter of time. He's got his career to consider."

"Aside from his excitement over the Big Bend project, I didn't see the kind of ambition you're talking about. Certainly not anything that would keep him from focusing on his family."

Chloe sniffed. "Family?"

"Yes." Laurel sat down next to her. "It's obvious to everyone but you that Nick chose to give as much time to you and Josh as that project. Almost since he got here."

Chloe shook her head. "But what about his job with Stockton? What about all those other women?"

"What other women?"

Chloe fidgeted, squeezing her eyes shut. "They all wanted him, Laurel. I could see that last night."

"And what did Nick do about it?"

She rested her head on the back of the couch. "Nothing."

"See?"

"For now."

Laurel cursed and stood. "Jeez, Chloe! You're being as foolish as I was."

She opened her eyes and slid her gaze toward Laurel. "What? You mean, with you and Jack?"

Laurel nodded. "Assumptions, babe. They suck. You thought Nick would leave when he found out about Josh. He didn't. You thought he would sleep with Krissy again. He didn't. Now you think he'll cheat on you. He's done nothing to make you believe that."

"What about my heart?"

"What about your heart? What's it telling you?"

"I love him. He says he loves me, but..." She could only manage a shrug.

"You told me to take a leap of faith, Chloe. Now

it's time to take your own advice."

"I want to believe he loves me. I want to believe that he's in this for keeps. But what if I'm wrong? What if it doesn't work out?"

Laurel touched her shoulder. "What if it does?"

It all hit Chloe in a rush. She did believe him. She had to trust him. She had to take that chance. "You're right."

Laurel smiled. "I know."

Laurel stood and went outside, muttering to herself. Chloe wouldn't argue with her. She couldn't think about this now. Her head hurt, her heart hurt, and she would just deal with all this later.

"Mommy?" Josh came over to her and climbed onto her lap.

"Yes, baby?"

"Is Nick really gone?"

"I'm not sure." She ran her fingers through his hair, hair so like Nick's, and sighed. "You like him, don't you?"

"Yeah. We had fun fishing with Uncle Jack, too. We were gonna use Nick's flies next time."

"Nick tied flies?"

"Uncle Jack showed him. He's pretty good, too."

Nick tied flies?

"You'll see Nick again, sweetie. I promise."

"Good."

"Let's eat," Jack called.

Josh scrambled down from the couch and ran to the table. Chloe sat there, feeling more adrift than she had after learning she was pregnant six years ago. Nick certainly looked like he wanted to stay here, like he wanted to be with her and Josh. But could she trust that? Was Laurel right? Could she take that leap?

She looked over at the three of them at the table and caught her brother's gaze. She saw the love there, but also that Butler stubbornness. Well, she had it too. And maybe that was enough to make her finally admit that she wanted everything Nick promised.

But was she brave enough to risk everything to hold onto the dream she'd only held in secret?

Chapter 20

Monday morning Nick jerked awake, his eyes gritty and his stomach sore. He'd managed to keep from bawling like a baby when he got home from Jack and Laurel's last night, but his dreams had been desolate and so sad his heart ached when he recalled the images. Josh staring at him in confusion, Chloe with that damn determination on her face, Jack and Laurel obviously concerned but powerless to stop what Chloe had set in motion.

He splashed cold water on his face, cupping his hand to drink from the faucet, and stared at his face in the mirror. He looked different from how he'd looked when he'd rolled into Cloud Canyon weeks ago. He was a father. He was a man in love with a woman who loved him but wouldn't let them be together. Scrubbing the towel over his face, he swore and threw it down. "The hell with it," he growled.

Grabbing up his cell phone, he called his father and told him he would help where he could on the Lake Tahoe project. He would just alternate his base of operations and see to both jobs. Joe seemed surprised and pleased, but Nick didn't bask in the approval as he'd expected he would. Wasn't that what he wanted when he'd first set out west on this scouting assignment?

He finished the call and crossed to the desk. He knew what drew him to the laptop and he clicked open the design program. He'd finished the plans for the house he'd envisioned for his little family, but now there was nothing to do with it but set it aside. Stubborn woman! If she would just open her eyes, she would see that they could have it all.

He closed the program. He couldn't think about it anymore. Last night he'd nearly bitten Fred's head off when he'd asked why his evening was cut short. Sure, Chloe promised he'd still see Josh. He would have never thought her the type of person to go back on her word, but wasn't denying what she'd admitted to him the same damn thing?

Saturday morning, he dragged himself out of bed like he had every morning of the past week. He'd avoided the café all week too, choosing to grab something to eat at the diner or making do on coffee and a muffin from the small bakery he'd discovered next to the sporting goods store. That girl, Josie, had waved at him through the window but he'd only nodded in return. He wasn't sure how close she was to Chloe and he didn't want to risk the chance of someone asking him about her. It would only twist the knife in his gut.

There was a knock at the door as Nick was getting dressed. It couldn't be Chloe, and only one reason was the growing distance between. It was the height of the café's breakfast rush. He walked over to the door and pulled it open. To his surprise, his parents stood there.

"Nicky!" His mother came at him, wrapping him in a hug. "Oh, it's so good to see you."

"Mom." He pulled back to look down at her. Crystal blue eyes stared back up at him. "What are you doing here?"

"She wouldn't stay away," his father said with a short laugh. "I wanted to see things firsthand and she wanted to see you."

They were both dressed for a day of antiquing or some other sort of day trip. His mother wore jeans with a thin yellow sweater and his dad wore khakis and a navy golf shirt.

"Did you go out to the property?" Nick asked them.

"Yes, and it's as amazing as you said," his father

said. "The pictures didn't do it justice."

Pride filled Nick at his dad's words. "I'm glad you like it."

"It's gorgeous, Nicky." She squeezed his arms and released him. "So. Tell me about Cloud Canyon and why it has a hold on you?"

Nick blinked. "What?"

She walked around the room and began to straighten the pillows on the bed and smooth the quilt. She was stalling, and he knew it.

"Mom?"

"You've been different since you've been here, Nicky. It can't just be the fresh mountain air."

"What do you mean?"

His father snorted. "Come on, Nick. There's got to be something else here." He wiggled his brows. "Maybe, someone else?"

His mother straightened. "Oh, you're not playing at that again. Please, Nicky. Tell me you're not."

"Playing at what?"

"The field, son," his father said. "Nothing wrong with fooling around."

"Joe, stop." His mother put her hands on her hips. "Nicky is too old for that."

Nick rolled his eyes. "Jeez. I'm not playing the field, Dad. And I'm not fooling around."

She smiled at him. "Good. Now, who is she?"

"Who?"

"The girl you're seeing," she said. "Your father said you're not spending much time on the Lake Tahoe project. And you're sticking around Cloud Canyon."

"That's true enough," Nick said.

"And there can only be one reason you're staying here, in addition to your project. You're seeing someone."

He looked away and his mother clapped her hands together. "I knew it! Joe, I told you he was seeing someone here in Cloud Canyon. Who is she?"

Nick pushed his hair back from his brow and blew out a breath. "Yes, I'm seeing someone."

"The realtor?" Joe asked.

Nick shook his head. "No. I'm seeing someone I knew before. In Reno."

Joe looked confused but his mother's mouth fell open.

"It's her!" she said. "The girl you couldn't stop talking about."

Had he talked about Chloe back then?

"What do you mean, Mom?"

"When you came back from Reno, Nicky. You were broken-hearted. I've never seen you like that, before or since."

His mother was apparently as sharp-eyed as any Butler he'd met.

"Yeah, it's her."

"Did you know she was here?" she asked.

"No."

She smiled again. "Then it's fate! When can we meet her?"

"Honey, don't bother the boy. Not everything is fate. Maybe they're just hooking up."

Nick groaned. "Please never say those words again, Dad. And I don't know about fate, but this isn't just fooling around, either."

"You care about this girl?"

Nick nodded. "I love her."

"Damn," Joe said. "Son, that's wonderful."

Nick blinked at his father. He'd always urged Nick to play the field, to cozy up to the wives and daughters of his potential clients and business associates. His parents did have a strong and loving marriage, though. Maybe the guy really did want Nick to settle down, even though he'd never once mentioned it. His mother, on the other hand? She'd been making noise about his singlehood for the last couple of years.

"I don't know what's going to happen, though."

"Why not?" His mother frowned. "How could she not love you back?"

Nick smiled. "I think she does, Mom. She's nowhere near ready to admit it, though. Again, at least. And, there's something else."

"Something else?" his father asked. "What?"

Nick took a breath and forged ahead. "We have a kid together. A son."

His mother gasped, and then burst into tears. "Oh, Nicky! That's wonderful."

"A son?" His father clapped Nick on the back. "Damn, that's something else. How old is he?"

"Five."

"Oh, five! When can we see him?" His mother swiped away her tears. "We want to see him."

"Yeah, here's the thing. I'm not really sure if Chloe would like that."

"Why not?" she asked.

"We're just making our way back together, Mom. I've only been with our son a few times. And right now, she's put up walls again."

"Knock 'em down, son," Joe said. "You're a builder. I bet you can find the easiest way to do it."

Nick shook his head. "Not this time. I'm not even sure she'll let me see Josh again."

"Josh?" His mother smiled again. "What an adorable name. What does he look like?"

Nick couldn't help but smile. "He looks like me."

His mother clasped her hands again. "Oh, he must be beautiful!"

"He is. He's a great kid, too."

She nodded sagely. "You love him too, don't you?"

His throat grew tight. "I do."

"Then what are you going to do about it?" his father asked.

"Honestly, I have no idea."

His mother sighed "But a little boy, Nicky. A child and a woman you love? There has to be a way to make it all work."

"I didn't know about Josh, Mom. From the beginning."

"Why the hell didn't she tell you?" his father asked.

"I… Our time in Reno didn't end so great."

"That's the past, Nicky. You love her and you have a little boy together."

His mother's words were both simple and true, but he and Chloe had a lot to work out if they were going to work. He knew one thing for sure. He wanted both of them in his life.

"Let's go grab something to eat," his father said. "We saw a café on our way here that looks pretty good."

Nick's mind worked. Josh wasn't usually in the café during lunchtime. And he wanted to introduce Chloe to his parents.

"Yeah, the café is great. It's also Chloe's. I don't think we should go there."

"It's Chloe's, hmm?" His mother's brows rose.

"Then that settles it."

"You can't ask about Josh, Mom."

Her lips thinned. "I suppose. What if she brings him up?"

Nick smiled at his mother. "Then all bets are off."

"Spoken like a Reno boy." Joe laughed and slapped him on the back again. "Let's go, then."

He followed his parents' Land Rover in his truck, silently praying that Chloe wouldn't be pissed off at him for just showing up with his folks. He parked behind them, watching as his mother and father stepped out onto the walk and gazed up and down at the shopping center. He joined them in front of the café.

"Pretty rustic," his father said.

"I like it," his mother put in. "It's charming. And is that an antique shop?"

"Yes. Um, Chloe's mother owns it."

His mother blinked. "This is a real family operation, isn't it?"

Nick shrugged. "I'm afraid so."

She grinned. "I like that, Nick. That means that little Josh had family around him growing up."

311

"I know, but please don't mention him?"

Her lips thinned again. "Fine. Let's go see your Chloe."

He rolled his eyes. "Jeez, Mom."

"Keep it on the downlow," his father said.

The downlow? Had his father been watching too much reality TV?

"Yeah, let's go grab breakfast."

The little bell jingled above the door as Nick waved his parents in before him.

"Hello, and welcome," Chloe said. She was smiling wide at the newcomers, at least until she spotted Nick behind them. "Oh."

"Hello," he managed to choke out.

***

Chloe froze as she drank Nick in. Oh, he looked good. She'd missed him so much this past week. But she'd taken a stand and, even though she wanted to follow Laurel's advice, she just wasn't ready to take that leap of faith just yet.

"Good morning," she said to the smartly-dressed older couple with Nick.

"Chloe, these are my parents. Joe and Sharon Stockton."

Oh, of course they were. She could see bits of Nick and of Josh in both of them.

"It's very nice to meet you."

Nick's mother eyed her closely, with as much interest as her mother and aunt had ever exhibited. "Nice to meet you, Chloe."

The woman's gaze then darted around the café, and Chloe knew she was looking for Josh. Darn Nick, anyway. She turned away and shakily waved them toward the closest vacant table.

"Please, take a seat. Someone will be right with you."

And with that, she escaped to the back counter. Jeanine stepped close to her, leaning on the counter. "So those are his parents, huh? Think they're here to see Josh?"

She automatically shushed her, and then shook her head. "Am I to assume that the cat is out of the bag?"

Jeanine laughed. "Dude, the cat was out the first time anybody saw the two of them together."

Chloe nodded. "Yeah. Thank God Jack took Josh

fishing this morning."

"So is this the big meet-the-parents thing?"

Chloe gasped. "God, no! I don't think this is anything like that. Not after we… We're not exactly…"

Jeanine snorted. "Yeah, you've been dragging yourself around this past week, Chloe." She held up her hands. "It's none of my business. I'm no Butler." She laughed again. "Or a Bennet."

Chloe groaned as she remembered that the Bennet sisters were at their usual table. Turning slowly, she saw that the three of them had flocked their way over to Nick's table and were chatting with his parents like they were old friends.

"Could you wait on them, Jeanine?"

Jeanine shook her head. "Yeah, yeah. You big chicken."

Chloe shrugged. She was a chicken. She was afraid to even be near Nick, since anyone with eyes in their head would be able to see how crazy she was about him. He would see it, not that he needed any proof to that point despite their recent separation. But with his parents and the Bennets there? No way.

She took another look around the café and saw that the morning rush was just about over. Cursing herself for the coward she was, she ducked out the back of the café and headed to her mother's.

Before she'd taken three steps into the back of the shop, her mother was on her.

"So they're Nick's parents?"

Chloe nodded. "Yes. I don't know if he brought them here or if it was a spur of the moment thing, but at least Josh wasn't there."

"Would that have been the end of the world, Chloe?"

"No, Mom. But it would have opened up a conversation that I'm just not ready for."

"Maybe it's time you thought about someone else then."

Chloe gasped. Her mother was wearing her best stern expression, but her eyes were soft. She couldn't fault her mother for her concern. Not when she knew the motivation behind it.

"Mom, I don't know what to do." She sank into the little chair Josh used when her mother watched him. "I know Josh and Nick deserve to spend time with each other."

"So do his parents."

Her head jerked up. "I never really thought about his parents."

"Honey, I don't know what I would do if I wasn't able to see Josh as much as I wanted to. If they know about him, don't you think they might feel the same?"

"Yes, I suppose they might."

"I'm sure of it." Her mother crossed her arms. "Chloe Butler, you have made a mess of things."

Chloe found a smile. "I know I have. First with Nick, and now with his parents."

Her mother clicked her tongue and crouched down beside her. "Now, before you don a hair shirt or parade around Cloud Canyon with a scarlet letter on your chest, think for a minute."

"About?"

"About how you can make things right. Do you love Nick?"

She began to object, and then gave a small nod. "I do. I'm a fool."

Her mother stood, grabbing Chloe's hand to pull her to her feet. "My girl, I never raised a fool, so I won't have you turning into one now."

"Okay, okay." She took in a breath. "Laurel told me to take a leap of faith."

"Oh? I've always liked that girl. Are you going to?"

"I'm not sure."

"Chloe, I've never know you to waffle."

"Mom, I don't even know who I am anymore."

Her mother wrapped her in her arms and for a long moment Chloe took the comfort she offered.

"You're Josh's mother, Chloe." She dropped a kiss on her brow. "You're my daughter and Jack's sister. And you're the woman who loves Nick Stockton."

Chloe pulled back and looked his mother in the eye. "You forgot one thing, Mom."

"What's that?"

"I'm a Butler."

Her mother smiled now. "And Butler's are stubborn."

"Yeah, we are."

Chapter 21

The next Monday, after spending the loneliest week in his memory except for his parents' surprise visit, he set out for Krissy's office to look over the papers for the Lake Tahoe project. At this point, it was better to just bury himself in work and stuff his feelings down deep. He'd never had a problem doing just that, not when his father spent too much time at work and too little time with his son. Not with any of the women he'd been involved with over the years. Besides, only with Chloe had he ever felt such deep, strong emotions. In Reno, sure. He'd been too young and stupid to recognize it then, though. And now? He loved Chloe, she loved him, but with what she'd said last week at Jack's there was no way she'd ever give them a chance to find out just how great they would be together. She'd just about chilled him out Saturday morning at the café. Being able to have a relationship with Josh would be amazing, but without Chloe his glass felt half-empty.

Leaving his room at the Treetop, he made his way past the café to Mountain Realty, unable to keep from peering through the window for a glimpse of Chloe as he passed. He snorted. "Jackass," he cursed himself.

Krissy greeted him in the lobby with a wide smile on her face. He didn't miss the concern in her eyes, though. Well if she was with Bo Butler, the guy with the biggest mouth in Cloud Canyon, no doubt she knew that Chloe had kicked him to the curb.

"Hey, Nick."

"Hey."

Nick didn't add anything else, and she finally cleared her expression and put on her business face. "Come back to my office."

He followed her and sat as she placed the papers on the desk between them. He looked them over, found a few places where wording might be clarified or reworded, and within the hour they were finished.

"Well, that should do it," he said, capping her pen and placing it on the desk. "I'm heading back to Reno but I'll still be in touch."

"What? Why?" Her eyes went wide and she nodded. "Chloe."

Her name jabbed at his already-sore heart. "Yeah."

"But Bo said... I guess things didn't work out?"

"No."

"When are you leaving?"

He shrugged. Truth was he wasn't even sure but he knew he couldn't spend another week like this past one, avoiding the café, fighting the urge to drive past her house hoping to catch a glimpse of her or their son. Staying away from any stray Butler who might cross his path.

"I'll be back to check on the progress in Big Bend, of course."

Krissy's face was set, then she leaned forward and touched his hand. "Nick, you shouldn't go. You should let her know that what happened in Reno was nothing compared to what the two of you have. Heck, even back then I knew I didn't stand a chance."

Something flickered in the back of his mind. Krissy's words and actions in his hotel room in Reno all those years ago were now a little clearer. She'd come in, undressed and climbed into bed with him. And then… That was where he still drew a blank.

"Seriously. I mean, we didn't even do anything," Krissy added.

He nodded absently, and then her words struck him. "What?" Nick sat up straight. "What are you talking about?"

She blinked at him for a moment then gasped. "Oh! Did you think we had sex?"

It hit him square in the gut. His head took a second or two to catch up but then he saw that night with focused clarity. He'd never slept with Krissy. She'd wanted to, but even as drunk as he'd been he'd only wanted Chloe. "Oh, God." He slumped back in the chair. "We never did anything."

"Nope." Krissy's face grew red. "I was an idiot for trying anything with you. I suspected Chloe was over the moon but I wanted some attention, too." She smiled ruefully and shook her head. "I was a little out of control back then."

Nick rubbed a hand over his face. "All these years I could have been with Chloe. With Josh."

"I'm so sorry. I thought you knew, Nick. I would have told you that first day in my office if I'd known you thought we'd slept together."

"I was so drunk I'd blanked on most of that night. Only that next morning…"

Krissy nodded then brightened. "You can tell

Chloe! She must think we slept together, too. Tell her we didn't and she'll have to let it go."

It would ever be that easy. As much as he wanted to grab onto that line he had to cut bait. Or fly, or whatever.

"No. She wouldn't listen to me before. I doubt she'd believe me now." He stood. "Thanks, Krissy. I'll be in touch. Let me know if you need anything from me on the project."

"But, Nick—"

He just shook his head and left her office. Once back at the inn, his mind reeled as he settled back on the bed. He hadn't slept with Krissy. Even back then, his heart had known Chloe was the one. He went to the desk and opened the saved design of the house he wanted to build for his family. It was perfect. His eyes burned with unshed tears as he imagined the life he might have had with her and their son in the house he'd designed. It was made for them. All three of them, and whatever little ones might have come along in the future.

He gave Krissy a quick call and asked her to print up the plans he would email to her. He didn't know if he would ever get to show them to Chloe, but he wanted to have a tangible copy if only for himself. There was no way he would let anyone else build that particular house in Big Bend, though. It was meant for his family alone.

If Chloe and Josh wouldn't live in it with him, maybe it was better that it never got built.

*

Chloe wiped down the last table and let out a breath. Jeanine was long gone, and so were Ricky and Tom. It was nearly five o'clock and she had no earthly reason to hang around the café. Josh was at her mom's, thank goodness. He'd been relentless this past week, asking her about Nick so often that she'd nearly screamed. How had he gotten so attached to Nick in such a short time? It was like he somehow sensed a connection, which had been her biggest fear from the moment Nick had come back into her life.

She pulled out the nearest chair and sat. Nick had looked so hurt that Sunday at Jack and Laurel's when she'd denied her confession. Hurt, and angry too. According to what Jack had said the past couple of days, Nick was still in Cloud Canyon. She hadn't missed her big brother's disapproval, either. But since Nick hadn't tried to contact her she was sure that he was only sticking around because of the Big Bend project. She'd finally gotten what she wanted. Nick out of her life again, and for good.

"Keep lying to yourself," she murmured.

She rested her chin in her hand. She so wanted to take that leap of faith with Nick. She wanted to trust him with her heart. She loved him.

Someone knocked at the door and she started. "Nick?" she whispered. She rose and went to the door, taking a breath to calm herself. She unlocked it and pulled it open, struck speechless when she saw the person standing there. "Krissy?"

Krissy held up a hand in a tentative wave. "Hi, Chloe."

Chloe could barely make a sound. She hadn't spoken to Krissy in six years. And Krissy had never set foot in the café since it opened. Something big must have happened to bring her here. "Hi," was all she could manage to say.

"Can I come in for a minute?" Krissy asked.

Chloe blinked, then stepped back to let her in. "Sure."

Krissy stepped over the threshold. She'd obviously came from her office. She had a large bag hung over one shoulder and carried a soft leather briefcase. "Can we sit a minute?"

Chloe waved toward the table she'd been sitting at and Krissy sat, her back straight.

"What do you want, Krissy?" Chloe asked as she settled across from her.

Krissy stared at her for a moment, then sighed. "I have to set the record straight, Chloe. Nick and I never slept together."

Time stopped as Chloe tried to process what Krissy had just said. If she had said that she could now fly over the Sierra Nevada on a magic carpet, Chloe wouldn't have been more surprised. "What?"

She set down her bag, relaxing a bit in her chair. "Whoa, it felt good to say that."

"I… I don't understand. I found the two of you together."

Krissy placed her hands flat on the tabletop, apparently bracing herself. "It was all me, Chloe. Nick never invited me to his bed and he turned me down."

Chloe's mind worked over what Krissy said. She'd found them naked together in Nick's bed, that was true. What other conclusion could she have made? But what reason would Krissy have to lie now?

"If this is true, why didn't Nick tell me when he first came to Cloud Canyon?"

"He didn't know." Krissy gave her a small smile. "He was pretty drunk. I thought he knew what really went down that night. If I'd known he thought we'd been together, I would have straightened him out on that score right away."

Chloe studied her former best friend, seeing only sincerity in her expression.

"Why?" Chloe had to ask.

Krissy's eyes filled with tears and Chloe felt her own sting in response. "I miss you, Chloe. I was a fool and sometimes a bitch, but you were my best friend. I should have told you what really happened years ago, but…"

Chloe nodded. "But I wouldn't talk to you."

"I can't blame you."

Krissy swiped at her eyes, smearing her mascara. Chloe handed her one of the napkins on the table and waited while she wiped her eyes.

"Thanks." She reached into her bag and withdrew a portfolio. "Look, I was only supposed to make a copy of this for Nick but I thought you would want to see it too. So I made one for you."

She placed a folder on the table and flipped it open to reveal house plans of some kind.

Chloe leaned forward and studied the rendering. It was a gorgeous house. The plan had large rooms, thoughtful details, lots of storage. "What is this?"

"Nick didn't say as much, but I think it's a house he designed for you and Josh. All the other plans for the Big Bend project came directly from Stockton."

Chloe traced her fingers over the plans. It was so easy to picture Josh in the play room, herself in the spacious yet comfortable kitchen, even Nick in the great room. This was a family home. He'd designed it for them.

"It's beautiful."

Krissy shut her portfolio, leaving the folder on the table. "I thought you should at least have a look at it before he goes."

She tore her gaze from the house plans to face

Krissy. "Before he goes where?"

"He's leaving, Chloe." She stood. "He'll be back to work on the project now and then but he's leaving Cloud Canyon."

Chloe stared down at the image a few seconds more and then looked back up at her. "Thank you."

"I'm so sorry," Krissy said, her voice thick. "I know you can't forgive me for what I tried to do, but thanks so much for talking to me today."

Chloe covered her hand with hers. "It's okay, Krissy. We'll talk again."

Hope filled her eyes. "Really?"

Chloe managed a smile. "You're seeing Bo, aren't you?"

Hurt flickered across Krissy's face, surprising yet very genuine. "I don't know what we're doing, really."

Chloe set that cryptic answer aside and stood. They shared an awkward yet familiar hug and Krissy left the café.

Chloe sat again and studied the plans. Nick had obviously spent a lot of time on this house. It was beautiful, and just what she'd imagined her perfect home would be.

He'd designed this for them? For the three of them to live in as a family? A sob caught in her throat. He wanted a future with Josh. With her.

Nick hadn't cheated on her. She'd been wrong about him all those years ago, and she was wrong about him now. Nick was the man she'd hoped he was. He was the man she wanted to be with forever.

She jerked upright. He was leaving. Krissy said he was leaving Cloud Canyon. She couldn't let that happen. Not until she told him just how she felt about him.

Grabbing up the folder, she left the café and headed for the Treetop Inn.

Chapter 22

Nick stepped out of his room and went down to the lobby. Fred Bennet was at the front desk, a sad smile on his face as Nick handed him his key. "I liked having you around, Nick."

"Thanks, Fred. I'll be back every couple of weeks."

The man's eyes were sharp behind his glasses. "Only every couple of weeks?"

Nick nodded. "I'll be working in Lake Tahoe, too."

"Busy man," Fred said. "What about your family?"

Nick flinched at the question before meeting Fred's probing gaze. "My folks are in Reno."

"Yeah, I liked meeting your folks. Good people." Fred's baby-blues seemed to bore into him. "But I meant your family here."

Nick's heart twisted as he finally admitted it out loud. "I don't have any family here."

"Yes, you do," a lovely, familiar voice said from behind him.

Nick felt like he had to be hallucinating. He turned to find Chloe standing in the lobby, hesitant yet with a look of determination on her face. He recognized that glint in her eyes. Butler stubbornness. He never thought he'd be happy to see that expression again.

"Chloe."

She took three steps toward him and he caught her in his arms. "You can't leave, Nick."

He'd never heard such beautiful words in his life. He kissed her lips, her cheeks, her neck until she laughed. The taste of her, the smell of her, God it was like coming home.

"Wait!" she gasped.

He lifted his head and smiled. "I'm just so damn glad to see you."

She placed her hands behind his neck and gazed up at him with those gorgeous blue-gray eyes of hers. "You have family here, Nick." Her voice was breathy yet firm. "You have Josh, of course. And me, too."

His heart seized. "Are you admitting that you meant what you said that night?"

"Yes." She took in a breath. "I love you."

He let out a whoop and hugged her close. "Baby, I love you too. I told you that night, but you were a little out of it."

"Well, I'm never drinking again," she smiled. She held up a folder and he recognized his plans. "I had to show you this."

He recognized the logo on the folder. It was from Krissy's office. It had to be his plans for the family home he longed to create.

"How did you get that?"

"Krissy brought me a copy."

That surprised him. "Krissy?"

"Yes." She looked over at Fred, who was smiling ear-to-ear, and motioned Nick over to the far side of the lobby. "She also told me about Reno."

So she now knew that nothing had happened. "Oh. It turns out the apology you'd never accept was unnecessary."

She nodded. "I'm the one who should be sorry. I should have tried to find you after I found out I was pregnant, even if I thought you'd cheated."

"I shouldn't have let you leave, not before trying to figure all of it out. I was so stupid."

"We both were, I think." She unfolded the plan and held it up. "Is this really our house?"

"Yes. I made the plans for you and Josh."

"Well then, I don't want it."

"What?"

"I don't want it unless you live in it with us."

He ran his gaze over her beautiful face, seeing that spark that was pure Chloe in her eyes. "You're serious?"

"I love you, Nick. You're the man I've always wanted. Even when I was young and stupid, I knew that in my heart."

His heart and head felt so light he thought for a second that he would float up to the antique-tiled ceiling. He knew what he wanted. What they both needed to make their reconnection permanent.

"Marry me, Chloe. As soon as we can."

She bit her bottom lip, then let out a squeal and hugged him tight. "Yes! I'd love to be your wife."

Fred let out a shout from behind the desk and Chloe and Nick glanced over at him. "Ha! I have the best piece of gossip before my sisters can get a hold of it!"

"Feel free to spread it around," Nick told him.

Chloe touched his cheek and he looked at her again. "What about the Lake Tahoe job?"

Nick shrugged. "Stockton can handle it without me. I'm going to focus on Big Bend. Spending time with you and Josh means more to me than money or success." He grinned. "Although I just know this project's going to be big."

"I have faith in you. And I'm sure your father will, too." She suddenly stilled. "We have to tell Josh."

"Tell him?" He stilled, so hopeful but unwilling to set himself up for any more disappointment. "Um, everything?"

She nodded as she stroked his arms. "I think he's already starting to love you, Nick. He deserves to know that you're his father. And you deserve to be the one to tell him."

He took her hand in his. "We'll tell him together."

***

Chloe sat beside Nick on the ride to her mother's, her heart lighter than it had been in days. Nick pulled the truck to a stop and switched off the ignition, turning to face her. "Are you all right?"

She nodded. "I should be nervous about this, but it just feels right."

"Man, I'm so glad to hear that."

Chloe looked up at her mother's house, picturing Josh eating a snack or watching TV and completely oblivious to how much his life was going to change in the next few minutes. "He's never asked about his father, Nick.. Not once. I knew I would have to tell him someday, but I never thought…"

"You never thought we'd be together again." He shot her that gorgeous smile. "Chloe Butler, giving up some of that precious control. I never thought I'd see the day."

She laughed. "Take it. I think I'm a little tired of trying to keep everything straight in my life all by myself."

He cupped her cheek, tenderness in his eyes. "I'm with you now, baby. With you and Josh both."

His words gave her strength and her heart swelled. She gave a firm nod. "Okay, then."

They got out of the truck and went up to the front porch. She rang the bell, and then took Nick's hand in hers and twining their fingers together. She felt that connection, strong and warm, and she welcomed it. It didn't scare her in the least, and she felt that certainty again.

Her mother opened the door. She held her hand to her heart and let out a sigh. "Chloe, thank goodness. Josh keeps asking me—" Her eyes went round. "Nick?"

"Hello, Mrs. Butler."

She leaned toward them, holding the door close behind her. "What's this about?" Her eyes sparkled, like she couldn't wait to be in on the secret.

"It's just the best news, Mom." She looked over at Nick, who nodded his encouragement. "We're telling Josh."

"Oh, that's wonderful!" her mother said. "Josh has been asking me questions about Nick all day."

"Grandma?" Josh came up behind her and pulled the door open wider. "Nick! Mommy, why is Nick here?"

Her mother stepped back, pulling Josh with her. "They've come by to talk to you, Josh. Let them come inside," she added with a laugh.

Chloe and Nick came in and Josh hugged Nick's legs. "I thought you were gone, Nick. Mommy said you were leaving."

Guilt slashed through Chloe, but she fought back the feeling. "I was wrong, baby." She brushed her hand over his hair. "About almost everything."

"Come on over here, buddy," Nick said, leading Josh over to the couch in the front room. "You mom and I have something to tell you."

Josh looked from one to the other, his eyes narrowed. "Will I like it?"

Chloe let out a breath and sat beside him. "Oh, I hope so."

Silence filled the room, and Chloe could hear her blood rushing in her ears. Finally, Nick smiled at their little boy.

"Josh, I'm your father."

Josh just stared at him for a moment, then waved a hand. "Oh, I know that."

Chloe's mouth dropped open. "How?"

Josh tilted his head to one side. "I heard it today."

Chloe and Nick exchanged a look. "Bo," they said at the same time.

Josh nodded. "He was at Grandma's store and I heard him talking."

Darn Bo. This could have gone very badly, but she couldn't rouse any anger at the moment. "So it's okay?"

"Sure. I like Nick." He turned to Nick. "I'm glad you're my daddy."

Chloe hugged him. "Oh, Josh."

Nick wrapped his arms around the both of them. He kissed the top of Josh's head and then Chloe's lips. His eyes stared into hers and in that instant she felt everything fall right into its proper place.

Epilogue

Six months later

Chloe stood back from the service counter, running a critical eye over the coffee makers, cleans mugs and glasses and silverware. The napkins were neatly stacked and the café was ready for the next morning's rush.

"See you tomorrow, Chloe," Jeanine called from the front door. "Come on, Ricky."

"Bye," Chloe said. "Thanks."

The two siblings, bundled up against the cold, opened the door. "Your guys are here," Jeanine said over her shoulder as they left.

Chloe turned to see Nick and Josh step into the café, both of them stomping the snow from their boots. Josh looked adorable in his puffy blue down jacket that matched his father's, and Nick managed to look gorgeous even with a ridiculous knit hat pulled low over his ears.

"Hey, guys," she said.

Nick closed the door as Josh ran up to Chloe. "The house is coming along," he said, obviously mimicking Nick's words. "It's big."

"I know." She turned to Nick as he joined them,

leaning up on her toes to kiss his chilled lips. They warmed in an instant and tasted so good. She pulled back and smiled. "How was your day?"

Nick draped his arms around her. "Good. I'm glad I got them to put in that foundation last fall. It's colder than a witch's—" He stopped and glanced at Josh. "The house is coming along."

She clicked her tongue. "We're having Christmas dinner at Aunt Beth's next week. I hope you're ready for a Butler family holiday."

"Should I be nervous?"

She gave him a knowing look. In the three months they'd been married, the family had been nothing but welcoming to Nick. Of course, that meant meddling and sharing opinions and pretty much trying to make him into one of their own. He was a good sport to put up with it, and she suspected he enjoyed every minute of it. His parents were kind to her and they clearly loved Josh, but no one could hold a candle to the Butlers for the full-on family experience.

"Is Bo bringing Krissy?" he asked.

It was easier to talk about her now, since clearing

the air about everything that had—and hadn't—happened in Reno. She and Chloe were mending their friendship, taking baby steps, but it was still progress. Chloe wasn't privy to her secrets, though.

"I don't know what's going on with them."

"Do you think—?" Nick stopped himself and laughed. "God, now I'm doing it."

She caught his meaning and smiled. He pulled off his knit cap and Josh did the same. Their hair stuck up in spikes and she smiled. She smoothed down their hair at the same time. Josh ducked away from her touch but Nick stepped closer. "Chloe."

She knew what that tone meant, the love and passion it promised, and suddenly the air seemed warmer. They started to kiss until Josh tugged on her sleeve. "Come on, Mommy. It's pizza night."

Nick laughed and pulled on his hat, turning to put Josh's back on as well. "Pizza night."

She grabbed her coat, hat, and scarf from behind the counter and put them on before joining them at the front door. She locked up and they stepped out into the growing dusk. The sky was pink, the air crisp, and she realized she'd been a fool to deny herself this happiness for so long. To ignore the secret dream that had lived in her heart since meeting Nick in Reno. And since holding their baby in her arms for the very first time.

Now with Nick holding one gloved hand and Josh holding the other, she was blissfully happy to be a fool in love. There were no more secrets between them, only the reality of a future that was so much sweeter than any dream.

About the Author

JoMarie DeGioia is a bestselling author of Historical and Contemporary Romance. She's known Mickey Mouse from the "inside," has been a copyeditor for her tiny town's newspaper, and a bookseller. She is the author of nearly 50 Romances, and writes Young Adult Fantasy/Adventure stories and Paranormal Romance too. She divides her time between Central Florida and New England.

Discover other books by JoMarie DeGioia

The Bridgewater Brides series, including

The Heir's Treasure

The Viscount's Vixen

The Earl's Beauty

The Gentlemen Undercover series, including

A Hero and a Gentleman

A Hero and a Rogue

The Shopgirls of Bond Street series, including

That Determined Mister Latham

The Dashing Nobles series, including

More Than Passion

Pride and Fire

Just Perfect

More Than Charming

The Secret Hearts series, including

The Courtesan Countess

The Cypress Corners series, including

Cypress Corners Boxed Set

Finding Harmony

Taming Jake

Loving Cassie

Winning Ben

Showing Jessie

Seeing Shannon (Barefoot Bay World novella)

Dreaming Eli

Giving Chase (Barefoot Bay World novella)

Kissing Bree

Wishing Joy

Bugging Nate

The Cloud Canyon series, including

Chasing Dreams

Secret Dreams

The Gifted YA Fantasy/Adventure Trilogy, including

Gifted

Braunachs of the Dell series, including

Luke's Gold

Patrick's Promise

The In the Castle series of Historical Novellas, including

In the Lady's Heart

In the Baron's Bed

In the Knight's Chamber

Connect with me online

Twitter: https://twitter.com/JoMarieDeGioia

Facebook:
https://www.facebook.com/JoMarie.DeGioia.Author

Website: www.jomariedegioia.com